How Could He Have Known She Was A Virgin?

Grace was a grown woman, for crying out loud. It had never entered Rand's mind that she hadn't been with a man before.

But she hadn't. And though he wasn't proud of it, there was a part of him, that primitive male arrogance, that was actually glad he was her first. She'd said he'd made it special for her, but she'd made it special for him, too. Special in a way it never had been before.

He glanced over his shoulder at Grace. Her cheeks were flushed, her deep green eyes alert and sparkling.

Something slammed into Rand's chest. Lust, most definitely. But something more than that. Something that made him sweat.

There was no future for them, he was certain of that. But that didn't stop him from wanting her.

Dear Reader,

Looking for romances with a healthy dose of passion? Don't miss Silhouette Desire's red-hot May lineup of passionate, powerful and provocative love stories!

Start with our MAN OF THE MONTH, *His Majesty, M.D.*, by bestselling author Leanne Banks. This latest title in the ROYAL DUMONTS miniseries features an explosive engagement of convenience between a reluctant royal and a determined heiress. Then, in Kate Little's *Plain Jane & Doctor Dad*, the new installment of Desire's continuity series DYNASTIES: THE CONNELLYS, a rugged Connelly sweeps a pregnant heroine off her feet.

A brooding cowboy learns about love and family in *Taming Blackhawk*, a SECRETS! title by Barbara McCauley. Reader favorite Sara Orwig offers a brand-new title in the exciting TEXAS CATTLEMAN'S CLUB: THE LAST BACHELOR series. In *The Playboy Meets His Match*, enemies become lovers and then some.

A sexy single mom is partnered with a lonesome rancher in Kathie DeNosky's *Cassie's Cowboy Daddy*. And in Anne Marie Winston's *Billionaire Bachelors: Garrett*, sparks fly when a tycoon shares a cabin with the woman he believes was his stepfather's mistress.

Bring passion into your life this month by indulging in all six of these sensual sizzlers.

Enjoy!

Joan Marlow Golan

Joan Marlow Golan
Senior Editor, Silhouette Desire

Please address questions and book requests to:
Silhouette Reader Service
U.S.: 3010 Walden Ave., P.O. Box 1325, Buffalo, NY 14269
Canadian: P.O. Box 609, Fort Erie, Ont. L2A 5X3

Taming Blackhawk
BARBARA McCAULEY

Silhouette® Desire®

Published by Silhouette Books
America's Publisher of Contemporary Romance

SILHOUETTE BOOKS

ISBN 0-373-76437-5

TAMING BLACKHAWK

Visit Silhouette at www.eHarlequin.com

Printed in U.S.A.

BARBARA McCAULEY,

who has written more than twenty Silhouette romances,
lives in Southern California with her own handsome hero
husband, Frank, who makes it easy to believe in and write
about the magic of romance. McCauley's stories have
won and been nominated for numerous awards, including
the prestigious RITA® Award from the Romance Writers
of America, Best Desire of the Year from *Romantic Times*
and Best Short Contemporary from the National Reader's
Choice Awards.

To Melissa Jeglinski, the best editor an author could ever hope to have. Thanks for keeping me focused, for trusting me, for making me laugh and, most especially, for just being you. This one's for you!

One

———

Rand Sloan had a reputation.

In fact, depending on who you asked and their gender, he had several. If you were a man, then *bastard, hardheaded* and *bad tempered* were a few of the words used to describe Rand. If you were a woman...

Well, there were so many words. *Amazing. Incredible.* And certainly the most popular overall—*extraordinary.*

But if there was one thing that everyone agreed on, men and women alike, it was that Rand Sloan was the best damn horse trainer in the entire state of Texas.

At thirty-two he had an edge to him, as if he'd already done and seen more than any other man his age. On Rand, though, the lines that etched the corners of his coal-black eyes and firm mouth only added to his appeal. His hair, thick, shiny and black, fell untamed down his neck. More often than not, his strong, square jaw bore the same dark stubble. He never hurried—a fact greatly appreciated by the women who knew him—and he always carried his entire six-foot, four-inch, lean, hard body with purpose.

Self-control and discipline were critical to Rand. When a man worked with a wild horse, those attributes could mean the difference between a nasty bruise or a broken leg. Even between life and death. Untamed horses were inconsistent and unpredictable, a few of the animals even teetered on the precipice of insanity. But all they needed was a little coaxing, a little patience, and he could pull them back, give them self-respect. Make them whole again.

Perhaps that was why he'd been drawn to wild horses, Rand thought absently. Why he'd chosen his profession—or why it had chosen him. Because he understood what those animals were feeling.

Because there were days, too many, when he also stood on that precipice.

"Here we go, sweetheart," he murmured as he led Maggie Mae out of her stall. The mare nuzzled the front pocket of his denim shirt, looking for a treat. He gave the animal a thick slice of crisp apple, rubbed the blaze of white on her forehead, then clipped her bridle to a ring on the redwood post outside her stall. The horse was small, but feisty and smart, a pretty two-year-old sorrel who would be auctioned off with the rest of the livestock and equipment when Rand's mother put the ranch up for sale next month.

Ignoring the hot, San Antonio breeze that swept through the barn, Rand set about his work. Work always cleared his mind, gave him balance. Today he needed that balance more than he'd ever needed it before.

It wasn't every day a man found out that his entire life—or at least his life from the time he was nine years old—was a complete lie.

That Seth and Lizzie, his precious little Lizzie, were not dead. They were alive.

Alive.

That one word wrapped around his chest like a steel band and squeezed. Alive. His brother and sister were alive.

Dust swirled around him as he raked numbly at the old straw, then replaced it with new. After he'd read the letter this morning from Beddingham, Barnes and Stephens Law Offices in Wolf River, Texas, he'd shoved it into the back pocket of his jeans. He hadn't looked at it since, but he knew every sentence, every comma, every word by heart.

But only one sentence mattered to him, only one that kept running through his mind, over and over...

Seth Ezekiel Blackhawk and Elizabeth Marie Blackhawk, son and daughter of Jonathan and Norah Blackhawk of Wolf River County, Texas, were not killed in the car accident that claimed the lives of their parents...

There were dates and the usual legal mumbo-jumbo, requests to contact the law firm as soon as possible in order to discuss the estate. But what the hell did he care about an estate? Seth and Lizzie were *alive*.

Seth would be about thirty now, Rand knew. Lizzie maybe twenty-five or six. Over the years, Rand had never allowed himself to think about his sister and brother or the night of the accident. But there were times, late at night, when even a bottle of whiskey couldn't chase the persistent demons out of his head.

And then he would remember—the lightning bolt, the sound of screeching wheels and crunching metal. His mother's scream and Lizzie's cries.

Then silence. A deafening, sickening quiet that pounded in his ears to this day.

How many nights had he woken in a sweat, the sheets ripped from the mattress, his heart racing and his hands shaking?

Too damn many.

Even now, as he thought about Seth and Lizzie, about the letter in his pocket, his hands shook and his heart raced.

"Rand?"

Startled from his thoughts, he glanced up at Mary Sloan's soft call. At sixty-one, she was still an attractive woman. Her raven hair was peppered with gray; her skin looked healthy and tanned, with deep lines around her blue eyes. She looked exhausted, he thought. But then, she usually did. Ranching was hard work, long hours and little pay. In her twenty-nine years of marriage, she'd never known any other life.

Mary and Edward Sloan had adopted Rand Blackhawk immediately following the accident. Mary had always been good to him, Rand thought. Raised him like her own, loved him.

Edward Sloan had been another matter entirely.

"Are you all right?" she asked, and took a step closer.

His first reaction was to say that he was fine. That everything was fine. Isn't that what everyone had always done in the Sloan family, pretended all was well, when in fact, it was anything but?

"I don't know what the hell I am, Mom," he said honestly. Or even *who* I am.

Mary knew about the letter, who it was from, what it said and what it meant to Rand. "It's one-fifteen," she said after a long moment. "Are you coming?"

Was he? His hand tightened around the handle of the pitchfork.

"Yeah." He stabbed at a flake of straw and tossed it into the stall. For her he would. "I'm coming."

"Rand—" She took another step closer. "I—"

She stopped again, not knowing what to say.

Hell, he didn't know what to say, either.

"It's all right, Mom. You go on. Soon as I finish here, I'll be in."

She nodded, turned slowly to leave, then stopped at the sound of car tires crunching on the gravel driveway outside. They both looked at each other.

"Are you expecting anyone?" she asked.

"Not me. You?"

"No." Her eyes, which had looked so tired just a moment before, now simply looked sad. "I'll go see who it is. Maybe it's one of Matthew or Sam's friends.''

They both knew that was doubtful. His younger brothers, Mary and Edward's birth sons, had both left the ranch years ago. Like himself, they'd come home only yesterday. No one knew any of the Sloan boys were back in town.

Once again she turned to leave, and once again she turned back. "We'll talk later. All right?"

Rand nodded. He watched his mother suck in a deep breath, straighten her shoulders, then walk out of the barn.

He stabbed another forkful of straw and tossed it. They'd talk, no doubt about that. He had no idea what they would say to each other, but one thing was certain, they *would* talk.

Grace Sullivan pulled her rented black Jeep Cherokee in front of the two-story farmhouse and parked. Tipping her sunglasses up, she took in the name carved roughly on a strip of pine over the front porch: Sloan.

Finally.

She closed her eyes on a sigh of relief and cut the engine. She'd been all over Texas looking for the legendary Rand Sloan. Even if he didn't live here, maybe someone who did could help her.

If anyone lived here.

She stepped out of her car into the blistering August sun and slid her sunglasses back down to shield her eyes as she looked at the house. Its once-white paint had begun to peel, the screens were torn, and the composition roof needed repair. The flower beds had long turned to weeds and dust, and the corrals were empty. On the porch a wooden swing with faded blue cushions swayed slightly in the breeze.

Her gaze swept back toward the mile-long dirt driveway she'd followed off the main road. A cloud of dust still hung in the heavy air from where she'd driven in. The land was flat, dotted with cactus and thornbush, and stretched as far as the eye could see. Grace listened, but the only sounds she heard were a hawk shrieking overhead and the squeak of the wooden sign moving gently in the hot wind. The place looked and felt deserted.

Not that there would be much taking place in this heat at this hour on any ranch, she reasoned. Still, she would have expected *some* kind of activity. Maybe a ranch hand smoking in the shade of the large oak tree beside the barn, or a horse nuzzling a patch of grass. But she saw no sign of life at all. Not even the customary mangy ranch dog had rushed up to bark at her.

Not your typical ranch, she thought as she closed her car door and headed for the house. But then, from everything she'd heard, Rand Sloan was not your typical man.

"May I help you?"

Grace turned and saw the woman standing at the edge of the house, her expression wary but not unfriendly. She was a tall woman, Grace noted, slender, but not delicate. Her short, dark hair was starting to gray; she wore black slacks, a short-sleeved cotton blouse and black cowboy boots.

"Hello." Grace smiled at the woman. "My name is Grace Sullivan. I hope I'm not bothering you."

"Not yet you're not." The woman moved closer and offered a firm handshake. "Mary Sloan."

A wife? Grace wondered. Sister? She knew so little about the man. "I'm looking for Rand Sloan. Does he live here?"

The woman smiled, as if Grace had said something funny. "Rand hasn't lived here for fifteen years."

Disappointment stabbed at Grace. Not another dead end, she thought. She didn't have time for another dead end.

"Would you have any idea where I might reach him?" Grace asked. "It's important that I speak with him right away."

"Take a number," Mary said, then nodded over her shoulder. "He's in the barn."

He's in the barn? Grace swiveled a look at the barn, tried not to let her chin hit her knees. That simple? After dozens of phone calls and three wasted trips, had she actually found the mysterious Rand Sloan?

Excitement skittered up her spine.

"Is it all right if I go on in?" Grace asked.

"Help yourself." Mary walked past Grace and moved up the porch steps. The woman hesitated at the front door, then said over her shoulder. "But if you're from that lawyer's office in Wolf River, you best give him a wide berth."

Grace frowned. "I'm not from a lawyer's office."

Mary nodded. "Good."

The wooden screen door slammed behind the woman as she disappeared inside the house. Brow furrowed, Grace stared after her. Now *that* was odd, she thought.

But her excitement over finding Rand Sloan pushed the strange woman out of Grace's mind. Gravel crunched under the sturdy flat heel of her ecru pumps as she made her way toward the large, weather-beaten barn. She wished she'd had time to change her clothes earlier, but if she'd wanted to catch her flight from Dallas to San Antonio, she'd had no choice but to go directly to the airport from the board meeting this morning. The off-white skirt and jacket might fit in at the glossy, teak, ten-foot-long table at Sullivan Enterprises, but on an isolated, dusty ranch one hundred miles from The Alamo, silk and high heels were definitely out of place.

The story of my life, Grace thought with a shake of her head.

She quickly ran through her proposal in her head as she approached the open barn doors. From the time she was old enough to read and write, if she had wanted something, Patrick Sullivan had insisted his only daughter present her case in an organized written and oral form. When she was eight, she'd gotten Princess Penelope's Tea Party by demonstrating the usefulness of learning social skills; when she was sixteen and wanted her first car, she'd argued the necessity of independence and self-sufficiency. She'd used visual aids for that presentation. Even now, at twenty-five, she still had fond memories of that sleek, shiny black Porsche.

She pushed all thoughts of tea sets and cars out of her mind, then squared her shoulders and stepped into the barn.

"Hello?" she called out, hesitated when she saw the man bent over a stall in the corner of the barn.

When he glanced over his shoulder at her, her mind simply went blank.

Good Lord.

Grace had no idea what she'd been expecting. Someone older, certainly. Maybe middle-aged, with bowed, skinny legs, slumped shoulders and skin like crushed leather. Maybe a bushy mustache and graying temples. Your typical, well-worn cowboy.

There was nothing typical about Rand Sloan.

He was probably in his early thirties, she guessed, though there was something about his piercing black eyes that made him look older.

He straightened, pitchfork in his hand, and turned those eyes on her. Grace felt as if she'd been speared to the spot.

He was well over six feet, lean, hard-muscled and covered with dust. His jeans were faded, his denim shirt rolled to the elbows. Sweat beaded his forehead and dripped down his neck.

And then there was his face.

She thought of Black Knights and Apache warriors, could almost hear the distant drums of battle. The pitchfork he held in his large, callused hand might have easily been a lance or a sword. A dark stubble of beard shadowed his strong jaw. His eyebrows, the same dark shade as his hair, were drawn together in a frown.

His narrowed gaze swept over her, assessing, moving upward slowly, sucking the breath from her as he touched her with those eyes of his.

Her knees felt weak.

"Something I can do for you?" he asked in a raw, hot-whiskey voice.

Now *there* was a loaded question, Grace thought, and quickly dismissed all the options that jumped into her brain.

"Rand Sloan?" she asked, annoyed at the surprise in her voice and the breathless quality that accompanied it.

He stabbed the pitchfork into the ground and nodded.

"I...I'm Grace Sullivan. I've been trying to contact you for the past two weeks. You're a hard man to get a hold of."

Grace blushed at her words. What woman *wouldn't* want to get a hold of this man?

"Sometimes I am," he said simply. "Sometimes I'm not."

"You don't have an address or phone number and I tried just about—"

"Why don't you just tell me what you want, Miss Sullivan?" His eyes dropped to her hand. "Or is it Mrs.?"

"What? Oh—it's Miss. Grace, I mean."

He lifted a brow. "Miss Grace?"

"No." Dammit. There was that blush again. She rarely blushed, and now she couldn't seem to stop. "Just call me Grace."

He nodded, his expression telling her that he was waiting for her to answer his question.

And what was the question? Oh, yes. He'd asked her what she wanted. She had to think a minute to pull her thoughts together.

"I'm from the Edgewater Animal Management and Adoption Foundation," she finally managed. "Maybe you've heard of us. We rescue wild horses and care for them until they can be adopted out. We'd like to hire you to round up some stray mustangs in Black River Canyon and bring them out."

"You went to a lot of trouble, Grace." He turned his back to her and stabbed another flake of straw. "My answer is no."

No? Just like that? *No?*

Grace stared at him, did her best not to notice the firm backside he'd turned toward her.

"We'll pay you very well, Mr. Sloan, plus all expenses and travel costs." She stepped closer, and the scent of fresh straw, horse and sweat-covered male assailed her senses. Strangely, the combination was not at all unpleasant.

"You'll have to find someone else."

He continued to work, his muscles rippling as he tossed another forkful of straw into the stall.

She'd met some difficult people before, Grace thought in annoyance, but Rand Sloan took the prize.

"I don't want anyone else." She moved beside him, refusing to be ignored. "I want you."

Rand straightened and leveled his gaze on Miss Grace Sullivan. In a different situation, he might have taken the woman's comment and carried their conversation in a different, more interesting direction. But this was not the day, and—he took in her light-colored silk suit and heels and caught the scent of her expensive perfume—this was not the woman.

Not that she hadn't caught his attention in the looks department. That thick, tousled, auburn hair of hers was enough to catch any man's eye. It was the kind of hair a man could fist his hand into, then pull that long, slender neck back and dive in. Her skin looked liked porcelain; her eyes were bottle green, wide and tilted at the corners, with thick, dark lashes.

And that mouth. Lord have mercy. Those lush lips of hers were meant for a man's mouth.

She had long legs—he guessed her to be around five foot eight—narrow waist, full breasts...

He glanced at the fresh straw, then at the woman.

What a damn shame.

"Why me?" he asked.

"Everyone says you're the best," she said. "This is a difficult job. Probably dangerous. I heard that's your specialty."

Another time he might have been flattered, and he definitely would have been interested. He'd always enjoyed a challenge, and the danger part made his blood race.

Another time.

He unclipped Maggie Mae's bridle. "You're wasting your time, Miss Grace."

"You're my last hope," she said quietly.

Her words, spoken with such intensity, made something catch in his chest. He didn't want to be *anyone's* last hope. Didn't want anyone to depend on him. He closed Maggie Mae's stall door.

"That's too bad." He tugged his handkerchief from his back pocket and swiped at the sweat on his face. "But my answer is still no."

"Mr. Sloan," she said when he started to walk away, then, "Rand, please."

He stopped when she said his name so softly.

"Could you please just give me a few minutes?" she asked.

"I haven't got a few minutes, Miss Grace." He glanced over his shoulder at her. "Now, if you'll excuse me, I have to go to my father's funeral."

Two

***

The sound of a car door slamming startled Grace awake. She hadn't meant to doze off, but after only five hours sleep the night before, the early-morning board meeting, the flight to San Antonio, then renting a car at the airport and driving one hundred miles, her eyelids had simply grown too heavy to keep open.

She rose from the comfortable easy chair in Mary Sloan's living room and looked out through the lace curtains. Mary and Rand had already stepped out of an old, dust-covered tan truck. A second truck, newer, deep blue with dual cab, pulled up in front of the house, as well. Two men younger than Rand, also tall, with dark-brown hair climbed out.

Grace glanced at her wristwatch, surprised that the Sloan family was back so soon from the funeral. The service must have been a short one, and the reception, if there had been one, even shorter than that.

Grace hadn't intended to stay at the Sloan house. As badly as she wanted—needed—Rand's help, she knew she couldn't intrude at such a difficult time. But it was a long drive to San Antonio, and after Rand had left her standing in the barn, Grace had knocked on Mary Sloan's door to ask for a glass of water before heading back to the airport. Next thing Grace knew, Mary had sat her down at the kitchen table and asked point-blank what Grace wanted with Rand. Grace had told Mary about the foundation and the horses, then Mary had insisted that Grace stay and join them for dinner.

Grace had politely turned down Mary's offer, but the older woman had refused to take no for an answer. It had been a long time since she'd had any company, Mary had said, and she would certainly appreciate another female in the house tonight.

The genuine concern in Mary's eyes, the sadness, made it impossible for Grace to say no. Since Rand had turned her down, Grace had nowhere to go, no one else to turn to, anyway. So why not stay a few hours if Mary wanted her to? Grace could only imagine how devastated her own mother would be if anything happened to her father. If Mary Sloan wanted female companionship, then it was the least Grace could do for the woman.

She looked up when Rand opened the door and stepped inside. He'd obviously showered and shaved since she'd seen him last. He now wore black dress jeans, a white shirt and shiny black boots. He glanced at her, unsmiling. Obviously, Rand did not approve of his mother's request that Grace stay.

Well, the hell with him. The man was just going to have to deal with it.

Their eyes locked for one long moment, then he boldly slid that dark, intense gaze of his all the way down her body, then slowly back up again. It annoyed Grace when her breasts tightened and, dammit, her nipples hardened. She pressed her lips firmly together. She decided he was crude and coarse and…just about the sexiest man she'd ever met.

"I heard you're staying for dinner," he said at last, bringing his gaze back to hers.

"Your mother—"

"Mind your manners, Rand Sloan." Mary swept in the house behind her son and moved past him. "I asked Grace to stay. A woman needs a breather with all that testosterone that'll be filling this house tonight. I need some feminine balance."

"Matt and Sam will be here," Rand called after Mary, then turned and looked at his brothers as they strode through the front door. "That should balance the femininity about right."

Surprised, Grace glanced at Rand. The man had actually made a joke, she realized. A sarcastic one, true, but a joke nonetheless. She wouldn't have thought he had it in him.

"I'll give you feminine when I'm picking your teeth out of my knuckles." One of the brothers walked toward Grace and stuck out his hand. "I'm Matthew Sloan," he said with a smile. "This is Sam."

Heavens, but the Sloan men were a handsome lot. Though Rand had darker hair and eyes than his brothers and his face was more sculpted, they were all rugged and tall, with killer smiles. Not that she'd seen Rand smile, she thought dryly.

"Grace Sullivan." She shook each of their hands. "I'm sorry about your father."

There was an awkward moment of silence, as there always was with condolences, then Matt said, "Thanks for staying. After looking at Rand's ugly mug all day, my eyes could use a break."

Rand frowned at his brother, but there was no malice in the look. If anything, Grace thought, it was the first sign of affection Rand had displayed.

"Matthew and Samuel," Mary called from the kitchen. "Get your butts in here now. I need help."

Matt and Sam excused themselves, leaving Grace alone with Rand. "I...I should go help, too," she said.

He took her arm when she started toward the kitchen. "In all the years I've known her, my mother hasn't asked for help in the kitchen once."

Confused, she simply looked at him.

"She's thinking we need a minute alone."

"Oh, I see," Grace said, then gave him a weak smile. "I'm sorry. I'm sure the last thing you want is to be alone with me."

"I wouldn't say that."

Grace felt her throat go dry at the flare of interest in his black eyes. She looked down at the hand he'd laid on her forearm. A working man's hand. Large, with long fingers and tanned, rough skin. Against her smooth, cream-colored silk jacket, the contrast was amazingly sensual. The heat of his fingers burned all the way through the fabric.

She really needed to get a grip on her hormones.

"Rand," she said carefully, "your mother asked me to stay, but I have no intention of intruding on your grief. Just forget why I came here and think of me as you would any other guest in your mother's house."

It might be hard to explain to the woman that his mother rarely had guests in her house, Rand thought. But it really wasn't anything that Miss Grace Sullivan needed to know, anyway.

"Samuel Sloan, you get your fingers out of that potato salad right now!"

Rand watched Grace's head snap toward the kitchen. At the sound of a loud *thwap,* those deep-green eyes of hers went wide.

"Shoot, Mom, someone's gotta make sure it tastes right," Sam told his mother.

"You saying I don't know how to make potato salad?"

Another loud *thwap!*

Rand heard the sound of Matt's laugh, then again, *thwap!*

"Hey! What'd I do?" Matt complained.

"It's for what you're gonna do," Mary said. "I saw you eyeing that cake."

"You hold her, Matt," Sam said. "I'll grab the cake."

"You so much as—" Mary's reprimand was cut off abruptly and there was a lot of hollering.

A good sound, Rand thought. When Edward Sloan had been around, the family rarely joked. The best times in this house had been when the old man was gone, either on a business trip or one of his hunting and fishing excursions. Fortunately for everyone, Edward took those trips often. It was the only time they ever really relaxed, the only time they could have fun like this without Edward hollering they were all making too much noise.

"Matthew Richard Sloan," Mary yelled from the kitchen. "Get your fingers out of that frosting right this minute!"

Grace looked at Rand, her brow furrowed with concern. "Shouldn't you go help?"

"Why would I do that?" Rand shrugged. "Unless you want some cake. I could probably grab it while they're all busy and be out the back door before they even noticed. My mom bakes a chocolate cake that could make a grown man cry."

"Chocolate cake, you say?" Grace lifted a brow and glanced at the kitchen. "With chocolate frosting?"

"Is there any other kind?"

"I suppose I could start my car and you could jump in," she said thoughtfully. "I'd expect a fifty-fifty split, though."

Rand felt a smile tug at the corner of his mouth. It felt strange to joke with a woman, especially a beautiful one. His entire adult life, when there'd been interest between himself and a woman, there'd been few preliminaries. There'd been the usual amount of flirting and silly banter, he supposed. But there'd been no pretenses, no long courtships. If he wanted a woman, he simply said so. If she wanted him back, then fine. If she didn't, then that was fine, too. He respected a woman's right to say no. There were always more women in the next town he'd drift to.

Not to say that he slept with every pretty female that came along. In spite of the rumors, Rand had always considered himself a man of discriminating— and careful—tastes. He was no fool, and he wasn't stupid when it came to sex.

He looked at Grace, watched those big, green eyes of hers widen at the sound of a crash from the kitchen. She wasn't going to be around long enough for him to give it a lot of thought one way or the other, Rand knew. She'd be gone after dinner, and he would never see her again.

And that, he thought as he looked at those gorgeous lips of hers and killer body, was a damn shame.

Unlike the worn and neglected exterior, the inside of the Sloan house was neat and tidy and clean. The furniture was utilitarian: a plain brown sofa and chair in the living room, maple coffee and end tables. A bookcase filled mostly with history and ranching books. No TV, no DVD or video equipment, not even a stereo, that Grace could see. Simple and practical and down to the basics, would best describe the Sloan residence.

It wasn't a cold house, but it wasn't exactly a warm one, either. Except for the dining room, Grace thought, where the family had gathered around an oval pine table to eat. She felt comfortable here, relaxed. Well, not completely relaxed. It was pretty difficult to truly relax with Rand sitting across from her, those incredible black eyes of his watching her. Not that he was staring. In fact, it seemed that every time she'd looked at him, he was intentionally *not* looking at her.

Nevertheless, she *felt* his eyes on her, *felt* the intensity of that dark gaze. No man had ever made her so…aware. Of him, of herself, of everything around them. The feeling confused her, made her unsteady. It also annoyed her that she was being such a nervous Nelly. Such a scaredy-cat. A big, fat—

"Chicken?"

Startled, she snapped her gaze to Rand. "What?"

"Would you like a piece of chicken?" He held a large platter of fried chicken in front of her.

"Oh. Yes, of course." She helped herself to a leg and smiled at Mary. "This all looks wonderful."

A person would have thought that an entire football team was coming to dinner instead of three men, Grace thought. Mile-high, fluffy mashed potatoes beside a tureen of velvety brown gravy; a heaping bowl of baby peas; golden, steaming biscuits with a tub of honey-sweetened butter. The smell alone was enough to make Grace's mouth water.

And when she took a bite of the chicken, it was all she could do not to groan. Mary's sons, on the other hand, were not subject to the same restraint. Every one of them, including Rand, expressed their pleasure with sighs and groans and enough compliments to make Mary beam with delight.

"Lord, I've missed your cooking," Matt said around a bite of biscuit. "When you sell this place and move, I'm just gonna have to follow."

"You're selling the ranch?" Grace asked as she scooped up an extra ladle of gravy. She didn't care if she had to do three extra miles on her treadmill at home. This meal was worth every calorie.

"She's moving to Sin City," Sam said. "Las Vegas, Nevada."

"I have a brother there," Mary said. "I haven't seen him in ten years. It'll be nice to catch up."

Grace listened while they all talked about Mary's move and their uncle Steve. It seemed odd to her that not once was there any mention of the funeral or Edward Sloan. No shared memories of their life together. And not one person had stopped by to pay their respects. It was almost as if the man had never existed.

"My mom says you're from Dallas, Grace," Sam said, interrupting her thoughts. "What do you do there?"

She glanced at Rand, who appeared intent on buttering a biscuit. She'd promised not to mention the wild horses, but she supposed it was all right to mention the foundation. "I work with Edgewater Animal Management," she said.

"I saw an article in the *Dallas Chronicle* about Edgewater Animal Management." Matt teased his mother by reaching for her already buttered biscuit.

Without missing a beat, Mary slapped her son's hand and kept on eating. "If I remember correctly, the piece mentioned its founder was the daughter of some mega-millionaire Dallas businessman."

"Probably some spoiled, buck-toothed debutante who wouldn't know the backside of a mule if it stared her in the face," Sam muttered.

"I do believe I would know," Grace said curtly and stared at Sam.

There was a long beat of silence, then Sam's eyes widened, and he had the decency to blush. Matt and Mary both started to laugh, and even Rand had a grin on his face. Sam took his knife and made motions of cutting his wrists.

"Hot damn, Grace," Matt said, still laughing. "Any woman who can put my brother in his place is the woman I want to marry."

"The fact that she's beautiful and rich don't hurt, either," Sam added. "Come on, Matt, I'll arm wrestle you for her."

Mary shook her head at her sons' nonsense while she offered Grace more chicken. Grace declined, shocked that Matt and Sam actually had their elbows on the table and hands locked, ready to wrestle. Never in her life had she seen anything like this. Dinner at her parents' house was always quiet and sedate, a five-course meal prepared by a cook and served by a maid on fine china and linen tablecloths.

Dinner with the Sloan family was like getting on a roller coaster at Six Flags, Grace decided. An exciting, fun, adventure-filled ride that took your breath away.

Rand was the only one that held back, she realized. Not that he wasn't at ease with his family. He was. But there was something about Rand that Grace couldn't quite put her finger on. It was subtle, but he was different somehow from his brothers.

He was watching her now, she knew, ignoring his brothers' shenanigans and focusing his attention on her. The intensity of his gaze made her shiver. The worst of it was, she couldn't look away.

"If you want that chocolate cake," Mary said to her sons, "you boys best get your elbows off that table. I taught you better manners than that. And, Rand, stop staring at Grace. You're embarrassing her. Just look at her, she's all red in the face."

Grace dropped her gaze. She hadn't been embarrassed, she'd simply been hot and extremely bothered. But she couldn't very well tell Mary that.

The meal finished in relative peace—relative being a very broad term when it came to the Sloans. Sam and Matt flirted shamelessly with her, plus there were more wisecracks and insults between the brothers. Even Rand jumped in a time or two, but for the most part he was silent and thoughtful, as if his mind was somewhere else.

When Mary rose to get the cake, Rand told her to sit right back down, then looked at his brothers. Matt and Sam went out the front door, with Mary wanting to know what all the fuss was about. The two younger Sloan boys came back in a few moments later, carrying a large, blanket-covered box. They set it down at their mother's feet and pulled the blanket back.

"Happy Birthday, Mom," Sam said quietly.

It was a thirty-five-inch color TV with remote control and picture-in-a-picture feature.

Mary stared, then blinked furiously, got up without a word and walked out the front door.

Bewildered, Grace watched while the brothers all looked at each other and smiled.

It seemed that Rand wasn't the only Sloan family member who wasn't inclined to show emotion, Grace thought.

"Let's set it up," Matt said, then he and Sam carried it into the living room.

"It's your mother's birthday?" Grace asked Rand.

"Sort of," he said cryptically and looked at the door his mother had walked out. When he glanced back at Grace, there was a grin on his face. "She just might need a little 'feminine balance' right about now," he said. "Would you mind?"

She had no idea what he was talking about, but if Mary needed company, then Grace would be happy to sit outside with her. She looked at all the dishes on the table, but he took her by the arm and led her to the front door. "Never mind the mess. We'll take care of it."

It was the second time he'd put his hand on her today, the second time her body reacted with a mind of its own. Grace opened her mouth, but hadn't time to speak before he'd opened the door, gently shoved her outside, then closed the door again.

The light from the living room window illuminated the front porch, but beyond the porch railing, it was pitch-black. Grace could see Mary on the porch swing, staring out into the dark. Grace waited, not certain if she was intruding or not.

"Come sit by me, Grace," Mary said.

Grace sat and together they listened to the loud *er-rick-er-rick-er-rick* of an army of crickets and the rhythmic squeak of the swing. Inside the house, the sound of Mary's sons talking and laughing in the living room drifted out into the warm night air.

"Rand doesn't mean to be rude," Mary said after a few moments. "He's having a tough time right now."

"You mean because of his father?"

"Heavens, no. There was no love lost between Rand and my late husband." Mary sighed. "But that's not what I wanted to talk to you about or why I wanted you to stay."

"Why did you want me to stay?"

"Rand needs a woman like you right now," Mary said.

Grace missed a beat on the swing, then picked it up again. "Excuse me for saying so, Mrs. Sloan, but I don't think your son needs anyone, especially me."

Mary laughed softly. "That's where you're wrong, Grace. I know my boy and I know what I see. He might not even know it yet, but believe me, he needs you."

"Mrs. Sloan—"

"Mary."

"Mary," Grace said, shaking her head. "I came here because I need Rand's help. He turned me down flat. The only reason I'm still here is because you asked me to stay.''

"And I'm glad you did.'' Mary patted Grace's hand. "It was refreshing to have another woman around. Sometimes living out here, without any woman friends stopping by for coffee or cookies, makes me forget I'm a woman myself.''

The sound of a baseball game blasted from inside the house, and Mary's eyes lit up. "Well, I suppose I should go take a look at what they bought me,'' she said matter-of-factly. "Wouldn't want to hurt their feelings.''

"Would you mind if I sat out here for a while?'' Grace asked. "It's been a long time since I've been away from the city lights.''

"Take your time,'' Mary said. "I'll make sure my boys save a piece of cake for you.''

"No easy task, I'm sure,'' Grace teased.

Smiling, Mary went back into the house. With a sigh, Grace settled back in the swing and mentally went over the events of the afternoon and evening. The Sloan family perplexed her. The sons had buried their father, Mary her husband, but Edward Sloan's name had not been mentioned once amongst them. Mary had plainly said that Rand and his father did not get along. Then the boys had given their mother a television for her birthday, only it really wasn't her birthday.

Rand needs a woman like you.

That comment from Mary had to be the most perplexing of all. Though there was no question there was chemistry between herself and Rand, Mary certainly hadn't been speaking of need in a physical nature. She'd been speaking of something else, something on a deeper, more meaningful level. Grace couldn't imagine what Mary meant, but it really didn't matter at this point.

Grace couldn't put it off any longer. It was almost nine and she needed to leave in a few minutes. It was a long drive back to San Antonio. She'd need to find a place to stay for the night, then catch the first flight back to Dallas tomorrow.

She knew she was leaving her last hope behind her, but she refused to think about that right now. Grace knew that she was still foolish enough to believe in miracles, and she also knew that it would take one now to save those mustangs.

Three

When Rand first stepped out onto the porch, he thought that Grace had fallen asleep on his mother's swing. With her eyes closed and her hands resting lightly on her knees, she looked completely at peace.

He told himself to go back into the house, to leave her alone and let her enjoy the quiet. But he quite simply couldn't take his eyes off her.

Long strands of soft, auburn hair tumbled around her serene face. Dark, thick eyelashes rested against pale, delicate skin. There was a regal quality to her straight, sculpted nose, angular eyebrows and bow-shaped mouth. He could picture this woman in a past century, smiling and waving to her loyal subjects as the royal carriage carried her through the cobblestoned streets of her dominion.

It amazed him that after a day of airplanes and cars and the hot San Antonio desert, she stilled looked so fresh and neat. Her white suit had no smudges or wrinkles. Even those low heels of hers appeared as if she'd just taken them out of the box.

He had a strong, sudden desire to put his hands on her and muss her up.

She opened her eyes, smiled at him as she stretched, and he wanted to do a hell of a lot more than simply muss her up.

Desire slammed through his body. Pure, primal passion. He struggled to get a grip on it, to wrestle the beast down. But even when he did, he felt it pulsing, breathing inside him. Waiting for him to let down his guard even the tiniest fraction.

"I brought you some cake." He clenched his jaw when she stretched again, wished to God he'd stayed in the house.

"Thank you." Her voice had a low, throaty quality to it. "But it wasn't necessary. I was going to come inside in a minute."

When he moved in front of her, Grace's eyes widened at the huge slice of cake he handed her.

"Good grief," she gasped. "I can't possibly eat all that. I already had to loosen the button on my skirt after that meal your mother served."

The thought jumped into his head that he'd like to loosen more than a button, then slide that skirt down those long legs of hers. Or better yet, shove the skirt upward and save time.

He felt the beast jump inside him again, and he fought it down. ''Well, if you don't want it...''

Her hand snaked out and snatched the plate. ''Mister, men have died for lesser evils than depriving a woman of chocolate.''

She took a bite, closed her eyes and groaned deeply. The pleasure on her face bordered on sexual. Rand groaned silently.

Damn this woman.

''Will you sit with me for a minute?'' she asked when she opened her eyes again.

Bad idea, Rand, he thought.

But he sat, anyway.

''I like your family,'' she said. ''They're...''

''Obnoxious?'' he supplied when she hesitated.

She shook her head and smiled. ''Bigger than life.''

''That's a new one.'' Rand settled back on the swing, watched Grace slice another piece of cake onto her fork. He followed that neat little bite all the way to her mouth and instantly went hard.

He dragged his gaze away, forced himself to stare into the darkness. It had been a long time since he'd sat out here on this swing, the first time he'd ever sat here with a woman other than his mother. He caught the faint scent of Grace's perfume, something light and exotic, then cursed himself when he dragged the fragrance deep into his lungs.

Annoyed with his wandering thoughts and overactive libido, Rand turned his attention to the sounds coming from inside the house. His brothers arguing over who got the bigger piece of cake and his mother reprimanding both of them. Just like the old days, he thought with a smile, only better.

Much better, now that Edward Sloan was six feet under.

His smile faded as he thought about the letter he'd tucked into the back pocket of his jeans. He'd been carrying the letter since he'd opened it this morning. He hadn't read it again, he'd just wanted it close....

...Seth Ezekiel Blackhawk and Elizabeth Marie Blackhawk...were not killed in the car crash that claimed the lives of their parents

...not killed...not killed...

He heard the sound of Grace's voice, but it took a moment for her words to register. She'd asked about the television set.

"It was Sam's idea," Rand said absently. "We all figured it was about time she had one. When my brothers and I were little, we'd go into Maiman's Department Store and we'd see her staring at all the televisions on display, watching whichever show happened to be on. She always had a look of such longing on her face."

"You mean she's never had a television before now?"

"Not for twenty-nine years." Rand rocked the swing into motion with the heels of his boots. "To quote Edward Sloan, 'They weaken a man's mind and spew propaganda.'"

"So your father—"

"Not my father," he said sharply. "Edward and Mary adopted me when I was nine, after my real parents were killed in a car accident, but he was never my father.''

The tone of Rand's voice alone spoke volumes, Grace thought. Mary had said there was no love lost between Rand and Edward. Grace was beginning to see more than a glimpse of that.

''Sam and Matt,'' she said carefully. ''Were they adopted, too?''

Rand shook his head. ''Sam came along a year after they adopted me, Matt a year after that. Quite the joke, isn't it?'' he said dryly. ''The doctors told Mary she could never have children, so she and Edward adopted me, then right away she has two kids of her own. Just goes to show you can't believe a damn thing people tell you.''

Grace had the distinct feeling that Rand's last comment wasn't directed at the doctors. That there was something else behind that dark, mysterious mask of his, something that had nothing to do with Edward and Mary or being adopted.

Something that was none of her business.

In the dim light, Grace watched the play of shadow on Rand's face. She had to resist a sudden and overwhelming desire to reach out and touch that handsome face, to run her fingertips over the hard set of his jaw and lay her palm on his smooth-shaven cheek. The thought alone made her pulse skip; she couldn't imagine actually doing it. Not only were she and Rand practically strangers, she was certain he wouldn't appreciate the gesture at all. Rand Sloan did not strike her as being the kind of man who wanted, or needed, comforting.

"You wasted a trip here, Grace."

Her hand hesitated on the bite that was halfway to her mouth. Well, now, *that* was certainly to the point, she thought. No, "I'm sorry," or, "It's too bad," or, "Wish I could help you." Just, "You wasted a trip."

"Hardly," she said lightly, then slid the cake into her mouth and licked the frosting off the fork. "This cake alone made the trip worthwhile, not to mention that dinner your mother made. She should open a restaurant when she gets to Vegas. She'd make a fortune."

There was a light in Rand's eyes Grace hadn't seen before. When he turned that light on her, she felt her breath catch.

"What makes these horses so important to you?" he asked.

He wasn't the first person who'd asked her that question. Her father had, her mother, every person she'd ever hit up for a donation. She'd never been quite sure how to answer. Wasn't certain herself that she knew the answer.

She looked out into the night, heard the distant howl of a coyote, felt the loneliness there.

"Was there ever something you felt," she said softly, "something that went so deep and was so important, that words simply fell short?"

When he said nothing, she went on, "My uncle has a ranch in Austin and I used to spend three weeks every summer there, riding and taking care of his horses. I've been riding since I was eight.'' She stared at the plate in her hands and shrugged. ''Starting this foundation just happened. One morning I was sitting at my kitchen table, drinking orange juice and eating cinnamon toast, trying to decide what to wear to my mother's hospital charity luncheon that afternoon. If my pink pumps would look better with my floral skirt or my leather dress sandals.''

Rand lifted a doubtful brow. ''Pink pumps?''

''Hey—'' she pointed her fork at him and lifted her nose ''—these were serious decisions in my life. A girl can never be too careful about her footwear.''

Grace could swear she saw a smile tug at the corners of Rand's mouth. Shaking his head, he drew in a slow breath, then said, ''Somehow I've missed the connection between shoes and wild horses.''

''While all these important things were going on, I was watching the television, too,'' she said. ''A documentary about an organization in Nevada that was formed to save a band of wild horses outside of Reno. I ended up calling the number asking for donations and spoke to a man named Mitch Tanner. He invited me down to see what their group was doing. I accepted, then came back and started my own foundation. The rest,'' she said, stabbing another bite of cake and popping it into her mouth, ''is history.''

Rand's gaze rested on her mouth. That light she'd seen in his eyes a moment earlier turned dark and sensuous. There it was again, that heat simmering between them. Grace felt her pulse stumble, but she steadied herself before she did anything foolish.

"Why are you here?" he asked, leveling his gaze back with hers. "Why me?"

"These horses—" she hesitated "—this roundup, is a little more complicated."

"Why?"

"The horses managed to break off from the main herd we've already rounded up and disappeared into Black River Canyon, a canyon that's notorious for flash floods. If they are still alive and we don't get them out soon, they will either starve or drown."

He stopped rocking and looked at her. "You're telling me you want to go into a dangerous canyon after a bunch of horses you aren't even certain are still alive? How many horses are you talking about?"

She swallowed hard. "Four or five, maybe six."

"You're kidding, right?" He sat up straight now, his brow furrowed. "You'd risk your life, or someone else's, to *maybe* save *maybe* six horses?"

"If they are there, and they are still alive, they haven't got a chance if we don't go down there and get them out." Grace closed her eyes. "Everyone else has turned me down. Told me it was a waste of time."

"They were right."

She opened her eyes again, narrowed them at him. "I refuse to believe that. You could do it. You're probably the only one who can. I've got two volunteers waiting to hear from me, two good horsemen who are willing to go down into the canyon with you and help."

"Mother Nature can be brutal. Life is that way sometimes and there's no way around it." He sighed, then added more gently, "Some things are best let go, Grace. Accept it."

She shook her head, not certain if her overwhelming disappointment was that Rand wouldn't take the job, or that he didn't believe in it.

Whichever it was, the bottom line was that he wasn't going.

He was right, she thought sadly. She had wasted her time coming here.

As much as she wanted to, she *wouldn't* cry. At least, not now. Later, after she checked into her motel room and crawled under the covers, maybe then she'd give in to the pain in her chest.

Forcing a smile, she stood and looked down at him. "Can't blame a girl for trying. I'll just say goodbye to everyone and be out of your hair."

He nodded, followed her into the house where Mary sat in front of her new television, a soft smile on her face as she watched a rerun of *Frasier*. The Sloan family stood, and they all said their goodbyes, then Grace surprised Mary by hugging her and wishing her well with her sale of the ranch and her move to Las Vegas. When Grace shook Matt's and Sam's hands, they flirted shamelessly once again, making her blush.

"I'll walk you to your car," Rand said when she turned to shake his hand, as well.

"That's not nec—"

But he was already holding the door for her, waiting, so she said goodbye one more time to his family, then walked outside.

She stopped on the porch and offered her hand again. "Thank you for your time, Rand. I—"

"I said I'd walk you to your car."

He placed a hand on the small of her back and guided her down the porch steps and to her car. Her body betrayed her by responding to Rand's touch. Grace pressed her lips together in irritation. Damn this man. He frustrated the hell out of her, in more ways than one. Heat shimmered up her spine; her skin tightened; her pulse jump-roped.

There was no other word for her reaction to him than pure, man-to-woman, simple lust.

She'd had boyfriends; she'd been attracted to men before. But she'd never experienced anything like this. She suspected she might never again.

There weren't very many Rand Sloans in this world.

Grace wasn't certain if that was a good or a bad thing.

He opened the car door and she half expected him to pick her up and toss her inside, he seemed so anxious to be rid of her. Instead, he hesitated, looked down at her in the dim light that shone from the house.

"I appreciate you being nice to my mom," he said, his hand still on the door. "Things haven't always been easy for her."

Or you, either, Grace almost said. "She's a nice woman. I'm glad we met. If I get to Vegas, I'll look her up."

He nodded.

But still he didn't move.

"Well," she said awkwardly, then held out her hand again. "Thank you again."

He ignored her hand. His gaze fell to her mouth; Grace felt her heart lurch.

His jaw tightened. When he turned away from her, Grace's heart sank.

She nearly laughed at herself as she stood there and watched him walk back to the house. Good heavens, what had she thought? That he was actually going to kiss her? That would be ridiculous. Absurd. They'd just met, and he'd made it clear he wanted no part—

Oh, dear.

He'd whipped back around toward her, a determined, intense expression on his face.

Her breath caught.

As he approached, she opened her mouth to say something, but the words were lost when he reached out and dragged her to him.

"I have to know," he said fiercely, then covered her mouth with his own.

Nothing could have prepared Grace for the onslaught of emotions swirling through her. His mouth was hard, demanding. A little angry, even. She tried to hang on to reason, but it seemed as if the ground had opened up under her and sucked her into a world where reason and logic simply didn't exist. She held on to him, not just because she wanted to, but because she *needed* to. Her legs had turned to the consistency of overcooked noodles.

His kiss shocked her, but what shocked her even more was the fact that she was kissing him back.

She felt the heat of his long, hard body press against her, smelled the masculine scent of his skin. His mouth moved over hers; his teeth nipped at her bottom lip, then his tongue invaded. She welcomed him, met every hot, wet sweep of his tongue with her own.

She thought what she'd felt for him before had been simple lust. How wrong she'd been. There was nothing simple about this at all. It was the most complex, most complicated, most mind-blowing experience she'd ever encountered.

And then it was over.

Just like that, he released her and stepped away. She had to reach for the door frame or she would have slid to the ground.

"Goodbye, Miss Grace," he said, his voice rough and husky.

Then he turned and walked not to the house, but toward the barn. Still struggling to breathe, she watched him disappear into the darkness.

Two hours later Rand could still taste her.

Even as he swung the hammer and slammed it down on the head of the nail, the taste of rich, sweet chocolate lingered in his mouth. The scent of her perfume filled his nostrils. The feel of her soft, full breasts pressed against his chest sang in his blood.

He had to be the biggest fool that ever lived.

He'd thought that one little taste of her would put her out of his mind. That whatever attraction he'd been feeling toward the woman would dissipate if he wasn't left wondering what it would be like to give in, to wrap himself around her and just let himself feel.

Big, big mistake.

As if his life hadn't been difficult enough right now, he'd had to go and make it even more complicated.

Swearing under his breath, he reached for another plank of wood and fitted it snugly against the one he'd just hammered in place. Eleven o'clock at night might be an odd time to repair broken stalls, but what the hell. He wouldn't be falling asleep anytime soon, anyway.

He appreciated that his brothers understood his need to be alone tonight. They knew about the letter, too. He'd shown it to them when it had first come. Matt had whistled under his breath; Sam had sworn softly. They hadn't asked him what he was going to do. They both knew that Rand would tell them when he was ready.

"It's a little late for all this sawing and hammering, don't you think?"

He turned at the sound of his mother's voice. She stood at the open barn door, wearing a red-plaid robe over simple, white cotton pajamas and her black cowboy boots. She had a bottle of Jack Daniel's in one hand and two glasses in the other.

He straightened, gave a shrug of his shoulders. "Needs doing. Now's as good a time as any."

She walked toward him, set the glasses on the saw-horse, poured a healthy shot of whisky in each one. "It's been a long day."

He set the hammer down and took the drink she

offered. They clinked glasses. He tossed his back, while Mary sipped on hers.

"Do you hate me, Rand?"

He frowned at her. "Why would you ask me a dumb question like that?"

She stared at her drink. "You should. Edward Sloan was a first-class bastard to you. He rode you hard, never let up, no matter what you did or didn't do. I should have stopped him."

"You couldn't have stopped him." Rand reached for the bottle. "Nobody could have stopped him."

"If it had just been you and me," Mary said quietly, "I would have left him. But after Matt and Sam came along, he never would have let me go."

In all the years they'd never spoken of any of this. Of Edward's strict rules and discipline, the lack of love in the house. The fact that Edward had openly hated Rand, a half-breed Indian boy who wasn't Sloan blood. Rand knew that if Mary hadn't been there to temper her husband, to balance out his meanness, Rand would have left long before he turned seventeen.

But there was one question he'd wondered all those years, one question that had never been answered. Rand asked it now.

"Why did he ever adopt me?"

Mary took another sip. "I wanted to adopt, your father—Edward—didn't. I got a call one night from a lawyer in Granite Springs who'd heard I'd been look-ing into adoption. He told me about you, that your family had been killed in a car accident and we could meet that night and adopt you immediately, without all the usual red tape and waiting period.''

"Didn't that strike you as odd?'

"I wasn't stupid. I knew it wasn't legal, but I didn't care. You were so frightened, so lost, and I fell in love with you the second I laid eyes on you. I told Edward if he didn't agree to adopt you that I'd leave him.'' Mary sighed. "I should have let you go to a better family, one where both parents would love you. But I was selfish. I'd hoped that Edward would come to care about you, learn to love you as much I did. I was a fool, and you paid for it.''

Rand shook his head. "It doesn't matter now. There's good that came out of it. I have you and Matt and Sam.''

"And now you have your real brother and sister,'' she said softly. "Seth and Lizzie.''

Rand sucked in a breath. Did he have them? At this late date, could he?

"You need to contact that lawyer in Wolf River, Rand,'' Mary said. "At least talk to him.''

"I'll think about it.''

Mary nodded. "And what about Grace?''

He looked up. "What about her?''

"You should go with her,'' Mary said. "Down into that canyon where those horses are. You could do a lot of thinking there.''

"Those horses are a lost cause,'' he said, and threw back another shot.

"The world is full of lost causes, son.'' Mary stood

and looked Rand in the eye. "Those are the ones that need help the most."

She turned and walked toward the barn door, then stopped.

"Rand?" she said without turning around.

"Yeah?"

"Thanks for the TV."

He couldn't help but smile. "You're welcome."

She took another step and stopped again. "Rand?"

"Yeah?"

"I love you."

Before he could answer her, she was gone. With a sigh he sat on the sawhorse and poured himself another drink, then pulled the letter out of his back pocket and opened it up.

"Dear Mr. Rand Blackhawk..."

"We can do it without him, Tom," Grace said into the phone as she paced back and forth in her motel room. She was still dressed in her pajamas, waiting for the coffee she'd ordered from the front office. She'd need it strong and black today. "I'll get the supplies today and meet you at the canyon's entrance in two days."

Grace listened as Tom argued with her over the wisdom of proceeding without Rand. They'd been going round and round for the past fifteen minutes.

"There's nothing supernatural about Rand Sloan," Grace said irritably. "Don't believe everything you hear. He's just a man, a good horseman, yes, but he's still just an ordinary man."

Liar, she said to herself as Tom continued to disagree with her. Rand was as far from ordinary as it gets. And she wasn't quite sure about the supernatural part, either.

Lord knew he'd put some kind of strange spell on her. Not only had she kissed the man like some kind of wanton, sex-starved hussy, she'd had dreams about him all night.

Hot, erotic dreams. His hands on her naked skin, his mouth on her neck, her breasts, and—

She blushed just thinking about it.

She got hot all over again, thinking about it.

Grace heard Tom calling her name and snapped her attention back to the phone. "Tom, we can do this. I know we can."

Dragging a hand through her loose, tousled hair, she looked at her wristwatch. It was already ten o'clock, and she wanted to be out of here by twelve, loaded with supplies and on her way to Black River Canyon. If she hadn't overslept, she would have been gone already.

"Listen," she tried again when Tom still refused to listen to her. "You and Marty are terrific horsemen and you're wonderful with the mustangs. You can—"

She stopped at the knock on her door. Thank God. She hoped the coffee came with an IV. "Hold on a second," she said into the phone and opened the door.

Rand.

She heard Tom saying her name, but she was incapable of words. So she simply stared.

He stood in her doorway, leaning casually against

the doorjamb. His jeans were faded, his black, collared shirt rolled to the elbows. He wore a black Stetson, black cowboy boots and aviator sunglasses.

She thought he looked like Satan himself.

"Mornin'," he said.

She felt, rather than saw his gaze slide the length of her.

And still she couldn't speak.

Tom was frantic at the other end of the line now, thinking something had happened.

"I—I'll call you back," she managed and hung up the phone.

"Sweetheart," Rand said in a rough, hot-whiskey voice. "You've got five minutes to get dressed or I'm coming in."

Four

Grace managed to throw herself together in less than the five minutes he'd given her. She jammed her arms into a white cotton sleeveless blouse, yanked on a pair of jeans while hopping around the room looking for her boots, then grabbed a hair clip and clawed it into the mass of uncombed curls she'd piled on top of her head.

So much for the refined rules of grooming her mother had raised her on.

When she opened her motel room door, she saw Rand leaning against her car, drinking hot coffee out of a large foam cup.

Her coffee, unless she missed her guess.

The steam drifted around that rugged face of his, and she felt her heart trip. When he lifted his gaze to hers, butterflies danced in her stomach. This man should be illegal, she thought. Or, like a pack of cigarettes, come with a warning label: Rand Sloan is hazardous to the health of women everywhere.

Sucking in a breath, she squared her shoulders and marched over to him. "Stealing a person's morning coffee is punishable by death in this state."

He lifted a brow. "The state of Texas?"

"The state of Grace."

He grinned at her and there they were again, dammit. Those irritating butterflies.

"Didn't your mother teach you to share?" he said, handing her the coffee.

"Not with men who show up unannounced at my motel room."

"You showed up unannounced at my place," he reminded her.

"Touché." She raised her cup to him, took a sip, then handed it back.

She wanted to ask him what he was doing here, why he'd come, but instead, she waited. She understood Rand was a man who did things his way, in his own good time.

The morning was pleasant, with a few wispy clouds in the blue sky. The air was still cool, but quickly warming up. Grace had lived in Texas all her life and knew how fickle the weather was, how quickly it could change. In the summer, though, there were only two degrees of heat—hot and hotter. And because that was too easy by itself, Mother Nature threw in a good dose of humidity to make it more interesting. Years ago

Grace had given up trying to dry her hair straight and had resigned herself to the thick, unruly mass of curls she'd inherited from her father's side of the family.

A man and woman stepped out of the motel room across from hers, said good morning before getting in their car and driving away. Three giggling teenagers, all girls, wearing bathing suits and carrying beach towels, headed for the motel swimming pool at the end of the parking lot.

And still she waited.

It worried her that maybe he hadn't had a change of heart about going to Black River Canyon. That maybe he'd come here for her. Well, not exactly for *her,* but for sex. After the way she'd kissed him last night, there was no question she was attracted to him. Maybe he simply had an itch, and he thought she might scratch it for him.

The thought made her stomach twist. She hadn't meant to give him the impression that she jumped into bed with strange men, or even men she knew, for that matter. She most certainly did not.

But the way she'd kissed him, without even the tiniest protest, could easily have seemed like an invitation for something more intimate. She could hardly blame him if that was what he was thinking.

Still, she couldn't believe he'd drive a hundred miles for a roll in the hay. Rand Sloan wouldn't have to drive far to find a willing woman. He wouldn't have to drive at all, Grace reasoned. A man with Rand's smoking sensuality could pick up a phone and have a busload of women come directly to his door.

No, he wasn't here for sex, Grace decided. Something told her, if he was, he would have already said so.

It annoyed her that she almost felt disappointed.

But as the realization dawned why he had come, Grace felt her pulse begin to race with excitement. He *was* going to Black River Canyon with her. He *had* changed his mind.

Her first impulse was to throw her arms around him and hug him, but she quickly fought back the urge. That, she knew, would be a very bad idea. Even though Rand hadn't come on to her, the tension still simmered between them, and she didn't dare risk everything by encouraging anything personal between them. Going to Black River Canyon with Rand was going to be difficult enough. Any sort of intimacy between them—even an innocent hug—would only complicate their already delicate relationship.

She wasn't even going to ask why he'd changed his mind. If he examined the reason too closely, she was afraid he just might change it back again.

They finished the coffee in silence, then he handed the cup back to her.

"We should get going." He glanced at his wristwatch. "We need to make Dallas before night."

How like this man, Grace thought. He didn't say, "If you still want me for the job," or "I've given this some thought and decided to go with you." He just said, "We should get going."

Well, she certainly wasn't going to argue.

"We'll need to go into town for supplies," she said. "I've got a—"

"Already done." He nodded toward the end of the parking lot to a dual-cab navy-blue pickup, complete with filled-to-occupancy double horse trailer.

And she thought this man couldn't still surprise her. She blinked at the truck, then looked back at him. "You don't waste time, do you?"

"Not once I make a decision." He pushed away from her truck. "You ready to go?"

His question hit her like a bucket of cold water. Was she? She'd been so sure of herself all along, so determined. Now that he'd actually agreed to go, she was terrified.

She sucked in a deep breath and nodded.

Five minutes later, after she called Tom and checked out of the motel, Rand followed her in his pickup while she returned her rental truck, then she climbed into his truck and they hit the road.

Late-morning sun shimmered off the unending ribbon of asphalt between San Antonio and Dallas. Rand was more than familiar with this long, lonely stretch of I-35. The dry, flat desert seemed to stretch forever, with cactus, tumbleweed and desert grass as far as a man could see. The landscape would change soon, though. They'd be coming into Austin before long, with all its cultural centers, skyscrapers and traffic.

But this was no sight-seeing expedition. Rand wanted to get to Dallas before it got dark, settle the horses and get a good night's sleep so they could be back on the road early tomorrow.

"Would you like me to take the wheel?" Grace offered. "It's only fair that we share the driving."

Rand pulled his attention from the highway and cast a sideways glance at Grace. She sat at an angle facing him, with one leg tucked neatly under her. She'd shucked her boots off when they'd stopped for fast food in San Marcos, then settled back and enjoyed a burger and fries. Her boots sat on the floor of the front seat. The seat belt cut across the front of her white blouse between her breasts and strapped across her lap.

Rand wouldn't mind being that seat belt right now.

He dragged his gaze back to the road and forced himself to concentrate on his driving instead of the woman beside him. But it wasn't long before an image popped into his head, one he'd been trying to push out of his mind all day—Grace in her pretty pink pajamas, her hair tumbling around her sleepy eyes.

The sight of her standing in her motel room doorway this morning, looking like she'd just slid out of bed, had caught him off-guard. Just like that, he'd wanted her. Wanted to step inside and close the door, slide his hands under that soft cotton and touch her everywhere.

He still wanted to, dammit.

Pulling his thoughts away from what he'd like to do with Miss Grace Sullivan, he asked, "You've driven a truck and trailer before?"

"Certainly," she said with a sniff. "Ranch House

Barbie came complete with a black pickup and horse trailer. Barbie and I went everywhere in that rig.''

He cocked his head and gave her his best that-wasn't-even-worth-a-smile look.

There was a glint of humor in her eyes as she brought her leg up on the seat and laced her hands around her knee. ''As a matter of fact, yes, I have, though usually short distances. I've transported several of the foundation's horses to their new adoptive owners.''

''How exactly does that work?'' he asked. ''The adoption process, I mean.''

''For the most part, the Internet.'' She leaned forward and searched the radio for a station that wasn't mostly static. When Travis Tritt came through the airwaves, singing about ''the best of intentions,'' she settled back. ''We also hold live auctions every two months at the Double S Ranch outside of Dallas where we corral and train the horses we round up or others that are brought to us.''

''Brought to you?''

''The horses that people don't want or can't afford to keep. Every horse has to be assessed and given a number on the adoptability scale.''

The adoptability scale. Rand's hands tightened on the steering wheel. He knew it was unreasonable, but it was impossible not to equate Grace's horses with what those bastards had done with him twenty-three years ago, and with Seth and Lizzie. They'd all been assessed and given a number that determined their worth to humankind. And while Rand understood that the system might work for horses, for human beings it was inherently wrong.

Rand knew that he'd been adopted out illegally; he knew it now, anyway. But he'd been told by the man and woman who had taken him away that night that his entire family had died, that he had been the only survivor.

Lies. All goddamned lies.

Why? His eyes narrowed as he stared at the long stretch of road in front of him. Why the hell would anyone do such a vicious, hateful thing—separate three young children after losing their parents and tell them their siblings were dead? How could anyone be that heartless, that cruel?

As if he didn't know. Money, of course. Money was the usual motivator for most men and women. Had there been some kind of black-market auction on his sister and brother? Rand wondered. They'd both been younger than him, certainly more adoptable. Especially little Lizzie. She would have been the child that anyone would want. Beautiful Lizzie, with her big blue eyes and shiny dark brown hair. She'd looked more like their mother than any of them, and the blend of Native American and Welsh had given her an exotic look.

The thought of his sister being sold to the highest bidder, like an unwanted horse, made him suddenly and violently ill.

He heard Grace calling him. He jerked his mind back to the moment, to his driving.

"Rand, what's wrong?" Grace asked, her voice heavy with concern.

"Nothing," he said through clenched teeth.

Breathe, he told himself. Slow, deep breaths.

"That's not true." She leaned toward him, her brow furrowed. "You're white as a ghost and you're sweating."

"I'm fine." He wiped at his brow with the sleeve of his shirt, willed his heart to settle back down to a normal pace. "Why don't you rest? We've got several more hours to go. Next time we stop, you can take over and I'll rest."

That way, there'd be no more talk. He could keep the demons away by concentrating on other things. He'd learned at an early age how to shut out the bad thoughts. The dark thoughts.

"Are you sure?" She watched him, a worried expression on her face.

"I could use some quiet," he said more firmly than he meant to, saw her pull away at his harsh words.

"All right."

She slid her leg off the seat and angled her back to him, rested her head on the back of the cushion. He could see the tension in her shoulders and back and had the strangest urge to touch her. To say he was sorry.

But he couldn't. Better to keep some distance, he thought. He'd already told her things about himself, about his parents dying and Mary and Edward adopting him, things he'd never told anyone else. Somehow, when he wasn't looking, she'd managed to get under his skin. Made him feel things he never had before. Things he didn't want to feel.

He wouldn't deny he wanted her in his bed, wanted his body to be inside hers. But on a physical level only. Not in his life, or in his heart.

That he simply couldn't let happen.

"Did you know that the best-preserved dinosaur tracks in Texas are close by here?" Grace asked while she and Rand studied the menu at Roger Bob's Rib House in Grandview. She'd read the trivia off the paper place mat on the table, but she doubted that Rand had noticed it. "The first sauropods tracks were discovered there."

"Is that a fact?"

"They also found tracks of the duckbilled dinosaurs," she went on.

He grunted, but did not respond, just kept staring at his menu and gave her no encouragement to continue. But then, he'd given her no encouragement to speak at all for the past five hours. He'd bluntly told her he wanted quiet while they'd been driving and though she'd admittedly been hurt by the cold shoulder he'd turned on her, she'd given him his space and his quiet.

But enough was enough, already. This lone wolf silent treatment of his was getting on her nerves. She was tired and hungry and she needed a conversation, dammit. With or without him.

"They were called theropods," she said with as much interest as she could muster. "Thirty feet long and twelve foot tall meat eaters."

"Well, let's hope they haven't ordered before us," Rand said evenly, and reached for the bottle of beer he'd ordered. "I wouldn't want to have to wrestle one of them for the last steak."

It wasn't much, but at least it was a start, Grace thought with relief. He'd been acting as if he'd had a sour drop stuck in his throat all day. And they said *women* were moody. Jeez.

They'd pulled off the Interstate less than an hour ago and found a small motel where Rand could care for the two horses he'd brought, a large-boned, dapple-gray gelding and a delicate pinto mare with the biggest eyes Grace had ever seen on a horse. He'd brought everything they'd need for the trip—canned food, drinking water and sleeping bags. He'd even brought her one of Mary's cowboy hats. It amazed her that he could be ready so quickly for an excursion like this, but at the same time, she had the distinct feeling that Rand was a man who was always ready to head out somewhere, always ready to move on.

Definitely not the type to stay in one place long, and definitely not the type to settle down.

She reached for the margarita she'd ordered and took a sip, then licked the salt from her lips. It had been a long day, and she needed something to unwind after spending eight hours cooped up in the cab of a truck with Rand. Every inch of that long, hard-muscled body radiated masculinity. He filled her senses. The earthy-male scent of his skin, the rugged profile of his handsome face, his large, callused hands on the steering wheel. And on those rare occasions when he had spoken, the deep, gravelly texture in his voice felt like the tip of a finger moving slowly up her spine.

If they hadn't stopped soon, she was afraid she might have thrown herself out of the truck. Or more likely, thrown herself on him.

"Rand Sloan!" A pretty blond waitress from another table hurried over. "You're a sight, cowboy. Where you been this time? Abilene or Del Rio?"

"El Paso," he said with a grin.

"El Paso! No wonder you been scarce as hen's teeth." The woman turned her big, blue eyes on Grace and stuck out a hand. "Hi. I'm Crystal. I'd wait for Rand to introduce us, but my Social Security check would probably get here first."

Considering the woman only looked about thirty, that would obviously be a long time, Grace thought. She smiled back at the waitress and shook her hand. "Grace Sullivan."

Grace couldn't help but notice that Crystal wore no wedding ring. And based on the way she'd greeted Rand, the two were very well acquainted.

And considering the amount of moving around he did, no doubt Rand Sloan was well acquainted with a lot of women in the state of Texas.

"Grace Sullivan." Crystal furrowed her brow, then her eyes widened. "I know who you are. You're with that horse adoption agency. I saw you on TV last week. That cute guy with dimples on Channel 8 news was interviewing you."

Normally one of the staff volunteers for Edgewater

Animal Management handled the PR, but no one had been available that day, and Grace had been forced to do the interview herself. She wasn't comfortable in front of a camera of any kind, but the spot on the news show had brought in a lot of donations, so she certainly wasn't complaining.

"Hey, Pinkie," Crystal called over her shoulder to the restaurant manager. "We got a celebrity here. Bring some free guacamole and chips out and make sure these drinks are on the house."

Grace felt her cheeks flame as several other people, restaurant workers and patrons alike, gathered around the table.

So much for having any kind of conversation or quiet meal with Rand, Grace thought. She could see the amusement in his eyes as he settled back in the booth and took a long pull on his beer.

Still, once she started talking about the foundation, explaining how the wild horses were rounded up and brought in, then adopted out, Grace forgot about Rand and concentrated on the growing crowd.

Rand, on the other hand, had not forgotten about Grace in the slightest.

He watched her, fascinated at the light that came into her eyes every time she talked about the foundation. There weren't many people who were truly passionate about their work, he knew. He'd been lucky. From the time he was five, he'd always known what he would do. He'd never even considered anything other than working with horses. He'd rather drink tar than put on a tie or a suit, or work indoors eight to five.

Handling and training horses came easy to him. People did not. Grace, on the other hand, was as easy with people as a duck swimming in a pond. Her face was animated as she rambled off statistics and talked about the horses and her organization; her skin literally glowed. When she laughed at something one of the local ranchers said, Rand felt something shift in his chest. When she took another sip of her margarita, then licked the salt from her lips, he felt something shift lower on his body.

Just that simple, innocent sweep of her tongue over her mouth made his blood heat up and his pulse pound.

When she did it again, his hand tightened on the bottle of beer in his hands.

Dammit, she was turning him on. Right here in front of a dozen people at least. He told himself to look away, to count backward by threes, but he couldn't get past eighty-eight before he was looking at her again, staring at that lush mouth still damp from her tongue.

He knew what she tasted like after she'd eaten chocolate cake; he suddenly wanted to know what she'd taste like now. A tangy mixture of sweet and sour, he was certain. And salt. Salt that would only make him thirsty for another taste. And another.

With tremendous effort, he dragged his gaze from her and glanced at the people who had gathered around their table. He'd been a regular at this restaurant when he'd worked a three-month stretch at the Rocking J in Waxahachie, a town five miles from here. That must have been three years ago now, he figured. Considering the number of ranches he'd worked for in the state, sometimes it was hard to remember what year he'd worked where. Sometimes he didn't know what year it was now, or where he was.

Or who he was.

That was the biggest question. Who the hell was he? Rand Blackhawk or Rand Sloan? He'd only been Rand Blackhawk for nine years. Could he go back?

Did he want to?

And Lizzie and Seth. Once they found out he was alive, would they want him as their brother again?

Could they ever forgive him?

He knew he'd never forgiven himself.

A burst of laughter dragged him from his thoughts. Dammit, he'd encouraged all these people to gather around Grace to give him a breather from making conversation. Now he simply wanted them gone.

Especially the guy in the white Stetson who'd been staring at Grace since he'd sauntered over from his own table across the aisle. Rand vaguely remembered him as a rancher who lived over in Brandon. Clay Johnson was his name, but as Rand recalled, everyone called him C.J. Last he knew, Clay was single with a couple of kids and looking. Apparently, based on the interest in the rancher's gaze as he watched Grace, the man was still looking.

As stupid as it was, Rand did not like it one little bit.

He'd never been the jealous type. He couldn't ever remember feeling possessive or annoyed if another man looked at a woman he was with.

Not that he was *with* Grace, he reminded himself. He might have kissed her, but that was before he'd agreed to work for her foundation. Their relationship was business now, and that's the way it needed to be. He needed to stay focused.

Oh, he was focused, all right, he thought sourly. On Grace's incredible mouth and long, curvy legs. Her tempting, full breasts that he'd love to—

He slammed his beer down on the table and drew a few looks from the group, including Grace.

"You think we might get our food sometime before Christmas?" Rand asked Pinkie, who had come out of the kitchen and was busy yakking with the rest of the party around the table. "Or do I have to go in the kitchen and get it myself?"

"Help yourself, Rand," Pinkie said, and pulled up a chair next to Grace. "Ribs are already cooked and sitting under the lamp."

That did it. Rand leaned forward and said in a low growl, "If I don't have my food in front of me in two minutes, *you're* gonna be under that lamp."

Pinkie sighed and straggled back to the kitchen, and seeing the mood Rand was in, the crowd scattered, as well, including C.J.

But not before he gave Grace his card and told her to call him if she could use his help with anything or if she were ever passing through.

Rand clenched his jaw so tight he thought he might crack a tooth.

"You all right?" Grace asked him with concern.

"I'm fine. Just fine," he snarled.

She raised an eyebrow, but didn't say anything, just settled back.

After a long moment of silence, she said, "Did you know that sauropods were plant-eating reptiles, more than sixty feet long, weighing thirty tons?"

"You don't say."

Rand suppressed a groan, listened to Grace while she spouted off dinosaur trivia and prayed this meal would be over soon.

Five

They arrived at the entrance to Black River Canyon late the next day, with barely enough time to set up camp before it got dark. While Rand took care of the horses, Grace gathered dried branches and bark from the surrounding red cedar and dogwood trees, piled everything into a small hole she'd dug beside a rock perfect for sitting on, then set a match to the leaves and twigs she'd layered underneath. It took almost an entire book of matches and several minutes, but when a flame finally sparked and the fire ignited, Grace gave a small yelp of joy.

She quickly bit her tongue and appeared nonchalant when Rand glanced over at her from where he was tying the horses to a nearby dogwood. He lifted a curious brow at her, then turned back to the horses.

Grace stuck her tongue out at him and made a face. She'd never admit it to Rand, but this was her first fire.

The truth be told, she'd only been camping two or three times in her entire life, but Rand didn't need to know that. She was certain he would never let her go down in the canyon with him if he was aware of her lack of experience with the rugged outdoors.

She knew what he thought of her, that she was a rich, bored city girl who had too much time and money on her hands. And maybe she was rich. She certainly didn't need to make excuses because her father owned and ran a large, successful steel-manufacturing company, or because she'd gone to the best schools and graduated with a business degree from UT. She certainly wasn't bored, and since she'd started the foundation, she definitely did not have too much time on her hands. She only wished there were more hours in a day.

She stared at her fire and smiled. Rand Sloan could just think whatever he wanted. What did it matter to her? She had to listen to her heart, and no one, especially some hard-nosed, temperamental cowboy, was going to stop her from doing what she needed to do.

High, jagged mountain walls surrounded them, a magnificent sculpture of carved red rock and sandstone. A slow-moving creek wound through a small stand of stunted oaks and the *ker-oke-ker-oke-ker-oke* of dozens of frogs filled the warm, smoke-scented evening air. Grace glanced around at the splendor of nature, at the wide, darkening sky and jutting cliffs and felt...full. She'd never been anywhere so completely remote before, and it was impossible not to feel the touch of something so much bigger than herself.

"Kinda gets to you, doesn't it?"

Her breath caught at the sound of Rand's husky voice close behind her. She'd been so engrossed in the scenery, she hadn't heard him come up.

She drew in a deep breath and nodded. "A person could forget everything here. The pile of bills to pay, the mountain of work, all the dozens of daily problems that fill a life."

"Like pink pumps or leather sandals?"

Grace heard the teasing tone in his voice and smiled. She didn't turn around, afraid if she did, the moment of magic they were sharing would be gone. After another full day's driving, with little more exchanged between them than a few grunts and an occasional token monosyllable from Rand, Grace was eager for conversation.

"Hey, a person can't help what they were born into," she said lightly. Then after a moment she asked, "What about you, Rand? What were you born into?"

He said nothing, and Grace worried that her question had stepped over that invisible line Rand drew around himself, the one that he never allowed anyone to cross.

A warm breeze drifted over them, carrying the scent of smoke and juniper brush. The sound of the crackling fire and the creek frogs faded into the distance, as if nature itself were waiting for an answer. The silence stretched, hovered between them.

When he finally spoke, she slowly released the breath she'd been holding.

"My father was Comanche," he said quietly. "My mother from Wales. She was an exchange student her last year at the University of Texas. My dad was taking weekend classes in horse husbandry. They met at the cafeteria, so the story went. She said he was staring so hard at her, she went up to him and told him to either stop staring or buy her a cup of coffee. They were married two months later, bought a small horse ranch in the town where my father was raised and settled in."

He paused, then went on. "One of my father's brothers was furious that my father had turned his back on his heritage and married outside the reservation and his own people. There was a huge rift in the family. I remember when I was eight and one Saturday I went into town with my parents. We were at the hardware store. This man came in and stared at my father with more hatred in his eyes than I'd ever seen in all my life, then he turned around and walked out. My mother told me later that was my uncle."

Though Grace had never been exposed personally to such prejudice, she wasn't so naive not to know it existed. It was just so sad, so incredibly sad. And the fact that it was family made it all the worse.

"Did you ever see him again?" Grace asked.

"Once," Rand said, his voice tight. "The night my parents were killed. He looked at me with that same hatred in his eyes, then turned his back on me, said something to a woman who was with him, then got in his car and drove away. The woman took me to her house, and two days later I was adopted by the Sloans. I never heard from or saw that uncle again.''

Grace couldn't fathom turning her back on a child, let alone family. Her insides twisted with anger at a man she'd never even met. ''And there was no other family to take you in? No place for you to go?''

''There was another uncle, but he had already died before my dad. My parents had led a fairly solitary life on the ranch.''

She turned then and lifted her face to his, saw the pain in his eyes. ''What about the funeral?'' she asked. ''Didn't you go to the funeral?''

''Far as I know, there was no funeral. Since my uncle was in charge, he had my father's body taken back to the reservation. I don't know about my mom.'' He looked down at her, frowned, then said softly, ''Hey, what's this?''

He reached up and brushed a tear from her cheek with his thumb. She hadn't even realized she'd been crying. ''I—I'm sorry for you, Rand. For your parents.''

He cupped her chin in the palm of his hand, continued to lightly brush her cheek with his thumb. ''It was a long time ago, Grace. Life goes on.''

She closed her eyes, felt another tear slide down her cheek. ''You were so little, you must have been so scared.''

''For a while. The woman who took me to the motel with her was nice enough, and Mary Sloan was a good mother to me. I got through.''

A child should do more than ''get through,'' Grace

thought. She had such a wonderful, loving family and she knew that quite often she took them for granted, something she suddenly felt very ashamed of.

With a sigh she turned her cheek into Rand's hand. The rough texture of his calloused palm against her skin, the scent of earth and horse and man, seeped into her senses.

He wasn't the only one who'd let his guard down, she knew. Perhaps it was the long, two days of driving, the fact that she was tired. Or maybe it was the spiritual and physical beauty of the canyon's entrance playing havoc with her mind. Probably it was a combination of both. But no man had ever made her pulse race with just a look, made her body respond to a simple touch. No man had ever looked into her eyes and made her feel that he knew exactly what she was thinking. Knew exactly what she wanted.

It terrified her that she wanted him. That he might know it.

There was so much more to this man than what he let people see. So much more than the lone, rough and rugged cowboy. He might have "got through," but not without scars.

His thumb, still lightly brushing her cheek, felt gentle and soothing. The hard edge around his dark eyes had softened, the tightness around the corners of his mouth had eased. What would happen, Grace wondered, if she pressed her lips to his hand, if she moved into the heat of his body and slid her arms over those strong shoulders?

She closed her eyes, and the innocent stroke of his

thumb on her face sent tiny vibrations of heat shimmering through her body. It seemed as if the air around them had turned heavy and thick, as if the ground underneath them was shifting and tilting. She felt the heavy, hollow thud of her heart in her chest, wondered if he could hear it, as well. Grace held her breath, felt the burn of Rand's gaze as he stared down at her.

It would be so easy to let go. Two people strongly attracted to each other, alone on a mountaintop, sharing a tender moment. It would be easy to give in to her feelings, she knew. What wouldn't be easy would be later, after that moment had passed and reality set in. That was the hard part. Or should she say the *heart* part. Because there was no doubt in Grace's mind that—for her—making love with Rand would involve much more than a joining of their bodies. Did she dare risk it, knowing that heartache was a certainty?

At the sound of the horses stomping their hooves, Rand dropped his hand, making the decision for her. Grace nearly protested, had to bite the inside of her mouth to keep from telling him that she wanted his touch on her. And more.

"I've got to finish with the horses," he said, his voice strained. "There's a duffel bag of canned goods in the trailer. Why don't you heat something up."

Grace might have laughed at his choice of words if her throat hadn't seized up on her. For the second time since she'd met the man, he turned and walked away from her, left her feeling as if she were on a tightrope, struggling to find her balance.

She watched him go, then let the breath shudder out

of her as she headed for the trailer on wobbly knees, to find something to "heat up."

Two hours later Rand sat on the rock beside the fire Grace had built and sipped at a cup of strong, black coffee.

This was the time of day he liked best. When the sun had just gone down and stars—millions of them—blinked in the huge night sky. He'd slept under those same stars dozens, if not hundreds of times, and each time he felt that same exhilaration.

That same peace.

It was probably the only place he'd ever found peace. Under these wide, open Texas skies. As far away from people and cars and paved roads as he could get. In a place like this, Rand could let himself relax. *A person could forget everything here,* Grace had said.

And a person could remember...

Rand Blackhawk, you stop fighting with your brother right now or I'll have your father hang both of you on a fence post and you'll eat your dinner there...

Hey, Rand, I found a garter snake, how 'bout you and me and Seth put it in Mom's bed and see how loud she screams...

How do you like your new baby sister, Rand? Her name is Elizabeth Marie. Isn't she the prettiest thing you ever saw...

He remembered the strong smell of lemon cleaner after his mother had washed the kitchen floor, the sound of his father's boots hitting the front porch when he'd take them off before coming in the house at night, his mother's stern look if her sons didn't keep their hands folded and eyes down when she said grace at the dinner table.

That was all he had left of his family. Memories. He'd taken nothing with him of his own that night, only the blood-stained clothes he'd been wearing. He'd been given new clothes, a new home, a new name. As if nothing before had ever existed.

That old, familiar ache spread across his chest. There were times he'd considered finding his uncle. Going to Wolf River and track the bastard down, confront him. Ask him why. But he never had. What good would it have done? Nothing would have changed. His parents would still be dead, and—so he'd thought— Seth and Lizzie.

But now things *had* changed.

Dramatically changed.

He'd have to deal with those changes when this job was done, but he'd made no decisions yet. Had no idea which road he would take or what direction. Since the night of the accident, Rand had sworn he'd never let anything frighten him again. And he hadn't.

Not until now. Now he was scared to death.

The fire popped, startling him out of his thoughts. He stared at the dancing flames, remembered Grace's excitement earlier when she'd finally managed to ignite that first flame. It was clear she'd never started a fire before, but if there was one thing to be said about

Miss Grace Sullivan, Rand thought with a smile, she was one determined lady.

One sexy, determined lady.

He'd always separated sex from business, never got intimately involved with any women he worked for or with. Women started to think they owned more of you than your time when things started to heat up. They started thinking picket fences, with little rug rat ranchers and ranchettes. He liked his life just the way it was. He went where he wanted, when he wanted, with whomever he wanted.

And that's how he intended to keep it.

Rand picked up a stone and tossed it into the fire, watched the sparks rain upward. Why was he having such a hard time keeping himself under control with Grace? He wasn't so stupid that he didn't know hormones were messing with his ability to stay focused and disciplined. He wanted the woman, he'd be a fool to deny that. But he'd also be a fool to act on his attraction to her. He'd been a lot of things over the years, been called just about every name in the book. But he'd never been a liar. Not to himself or any other man.

And never to a woman. He'd had a few short-lived relationships, but he'd been honest up-front. He wasn't the type to settle down. He never would be. He'd been on his own for too long to change now.

Grace was from that other world. That world where rose bushes grew behind picket fences, where bonnet-wearing babies cooed and home-cooked meals were on the table at six o'clock. The fact that she was rich only made it all the more complicated, but in the end it wouldn't be the money that would be the problem. It would be who she was, what she would need. What she deserved.

He'd already opened a door with her that he'd never opened with any other woman. Told her more than he'd ever told anyone about his past. It was time for him to close that door again.

That's exactly what he intended to do—keep his mind on his work and off pretty Miss Grace.

And then she walked out of the darkness like some kind of mountain nymph, a smile on her face, and his breath snagged in his throat.

She'd gone to wash up by the creek after dinner—dinner being a can of chili he'd brought and a bag of pull apart rolls Grace had picked up at a gas station convenience store earlier in the day while Rand pumped gas. She'd changed into a clean T-shirt, a fresh pair of jeans, and pulled her hair back into a ponytail. The smile on her face widened as she held out a paper bag.

"Dessert," she said, shaking the bag.

She sat cross-legged by the fire and dug into her cache.

He grinned and shook his head when she pulled out the contents—graham crackers, marshmallows and chocolate bars. He should have known it.

While she busied herself unwrapping and assembling everything, he watched her. Her fingers were long and slender, without rings. He wondered about that. Why she wasn't married, or at least engaged. She hadn't mentioned a boyfriend; he hadn't asked. He knew she'd made several phone calls to another volunteer named Tom. Her voice had softened every time he'd heard her speak to the man, and she'd turned away so Rand couldn't hear what she was saying. He'd say that was a strong indication that she might have something going on with the guy.

He was just making conversation, Rand told himself, when he asked, "So how long have you known Tom?"

She glanced up, clearly surprised by his question. "Tom?"

"Yeah, Tom. You know, one of the volunteers that's supposed to meet us here in the morning. That's his name, isn't it?"

"Yes, of course." Grace reached for a long, skinny stick she'd found earlier, stabbed a marshmallow and held it over the flames. "Tom will be here in the morning with Marty. They're both meeting us here."

She still hadn't answered his question, Rand noted. Was she being evasive? Well, fine, dammit. It wasn't as if she needed to explain anything to him, and it didn't really matter to him one way or the other, anyhow.

He gulped down the last of his coffee, waited for at least five seconds, then said, "So what's he think about you coming up here alone with me?"

"Who?" The marshmallow burst into flames. She yanked it out of the fire and blew on it.

Rand gritted his teeth. *"Tom."*

"He doesn't like it," she said, and slid the marshmallow onto a graham cracker already layered with chocolate.

"I wouldn't like it, either. If I were Tom, I mean."

Grace shrugged. "It's not his decision. It's mine. Here you go."

Rand took the graham-cracker-marshmallow-chocolate sandwich she offered him. He had no idea why, but she was starting to annoy him. "He must be a real understanding, patient kinda guy."

She laughed at that, and the sound rippled on the cool night air. "Understanding and patient would be the last words anyone would use to describe Tom," she said while she popped another marshmallow on the stick. "But I love him, anyway."

She loved him? Rand felt a muscle jump in his jaw. "If you *love* him, then what the hell are you doing gallivanting around Texas with me? How do you know I'm not some psycho socialite killer?"

"I am *not* a socialite," she said firmly, and stared at him as if he *were* psycho. "Rand, what's the matter with you?"

"If *I* had a girl, I sure as hell wouldn't let her take off for parts unknown, alone with some stranger." He knew he was out of line. But the thought of this guy she *loved* letting Grace run around and put herself in danger aggravated Rand to no end. "Sounds to me like Tom needs to find himself a little backbone."

Her lips pressed into a thin line. "Are you trying to make me mad?"

"Just making an observation." He took a bite of graham cracker. "It's your life, *Miss* Grace, but if I were Tom, I'd hog-tie you and lock you in the barn before I'd let you do something that just might get you killed."

"First of all," she said tightly, "you are *not* Tom. Tom is not a sexist, thick-headed, chest-thumping gorilla, which you *are*."

"Now wait a—"

"Second of all," she went on, "I checked you out carefully before I drove to your mother's house. I talked to at least six different men—and women—that you've worked for. If you're a psycho killer, then you've managed to fool every person who knows you, and you've hid the bodies very well."

"I was just making an ex—"

"And *third*," she cut him off again, "I'd like to see you just *try* and hog-tie and lock me in a barn, mister. I'm not as completely defenseless and fragile as you seem to think. I guarantee you that you'd come away singing soprano."

Good God. He'd unleashed a tigress defending her cub. Obviously, she *was* in love with this Tom guy. But that realization only irritated him all the more. "Look, just because I insulted your boyfriend doesn't mean that you—"

"*Fourth,*" she snapped out, "Tom is *not* my boyfriend. He's my brother."

Oops. He sucked in a breath. "Your brother?"

"My brother."

Damn. He felt like an idiot. "Well, why the hell didn't you say so before?"

"You were too busy criticizing and *making obser-*

vations about someone you don't even know to let me get a word in."

"You never once mentioned that this guy, Tom, was your brother," Rand said. "Why didn't you tell me before we set out?"

She yanked the marshmallow out of the fire, frowned at how black it was, then slapped it between two graham crackers, anyway. "Because I knew you'd judge him, just like you judged me. You'd think because he wasn't born with a bridle in his hand and raised on a ranch, that he wouldn't know what he was doing."

He stared at the graham cracker concoction she'd made him and shrugged. "Maybe I would, maybe I wouldn't have. You still should have told me."

"Why? What difference does it make to you who Tom is to me?"

Rand frowned. He didn't like that question. "Did I say it made a difference? All I said was that if you were my girl, I wouldn't let you go." Dammit, that wasn't what he'd meant to say. "Into the canyon, I mean."

The cracker that Grace had lifted to her mouth stopped midair. She looked up at him, her gaze steady. "I'm not your girl," she said evenly. "Or anyone else's, either. In fact, I'm not a girl at all. I'm a twenty-five-year-old grown woman. Your concern touches me, but I'm doing just fine, thank you very much."

"Fine."

"Fine."

They both turned their attention to the dessert Grace

had made. He watched those soft lips of hers nibble on a corner and felt his stomach clench.

As if he didn't know that she was a woman, for God's sake. Every thing about her was woman. The scent of her skin, the way she walked, the tilt of her pretty head. She sat here in front of him, those long, curvy legs crossed in front of her, with firelight shimmering in her auburn hair like fall leaves dancing in a breeze, and he sure as hell didn't need her to tell him that she was a woman.

I can keep my hands off her, he said to himself. I can.

She licked a spot of chocolate from the corner of her mouth, and he nearly fell off the rock he was sitting on.

"We should turn in," he said, looking at the two sleeping bags he'd already laid out beside the truck. "If Marty and Tom get here by eight, we'll need to be ready to move by nine."

"You go ahead," she said, still nibbling on her graham cracker. "I just need a few minutes."

He nodded. "I'm going to go wash up by the creek. If anything slithers your way, just give a call."

He saw the fear flash in her eyes, then she narrowed a look at him that said the only thing she saw slithering had two legs.

"I'll be fine."

He nodded and walked away. He glanced at Grace's sleeping bag, then at her stiff back.

...hey, Rand, let's throw a snake in Mom's bed and see how loud she screams...

Nah.

But the thought was enough to lighten his mood for the moment. He whistled all the way to the creek and back, then slipped into his sleeping bag while Grace still sat at the fire. He tipped his hat over his eyes, turned his back to her and fell instantly asleep.

Rain.

Icy cold, black rain. It pounded the windshield, the roof of the car. Rand felt his heart pound louder than the drum his grandfather had given him when he'd turned seven. "I think you should pull over," Rand heard his mother say to his father.

"Soon as the road widens around this turn," he answered.

Beside Rand, Seth sat still as a stone, his eyes wide with fear. On his other side, Lizzie sat in her car seat, sleeping. Rand's mother turned and looked at her sons. "We'll be fine," she said with a smile. "Don't be afraid."

Lightning.

Blinding white explosion. It hit directly in front of the car.

His mother's scream, and they went down into that black hole that Rand thought for sure was hell. The crunch of metal...Lizzie's cry...

Then nothing...

Absolute silence...

Heart racing, pulse-pounding, Rand sat. Darkness surrounded him. *Where the hell am I?* He felt a moment of panic, told himself to breathe slowly...

A dream, he told himself. Just a dream. Again.

"Rand?"

He snapped his head in the direction of the woman's voice.

Grace. It was Grace.

Relief poured through him. He nearly pulled her into his arms, had to clench his hands into fists so he wouldn't.

He stared at her for a long moment, waited for her features to clear in the dim light of the dying fire. She sat on her knees beside him, her eyes filled with concern. Shadows danced on her face and in her tousled hair.

"Are you all right?" she asked softly.

He still couldn't speak. The edges of the dream were still with him, hovering. He nodded, sucked in a breath.

She laid a hand on his arm and leaned closer. "You were dreaming."

"Go back to sleep," he finally managed, his voice hoarse and dry. "It was nothing."

"You're shaking," she said, and moved her hand up and down his arm.

Rand felt the heat of her skin seep through the light flannel shirt he wore. She smelled like sleep and fresh air and Grace.

He wanted her so badly he ached.

"Grace, for God's sake, just go back to sleep," he said roughly.

She shook her head.

Damn stubborn woman.

She moved in closer to him, kept rubbing his arm.

Rand ground his back teeth and closed his eyes. "Dammit, will you stop that."

He grabbed her by the shoulders and held her still. Her eyes widened for a fraction of a second, then her gaze dropped to his mouth.

His heart slammed in his chest, only this time it had nothing to do with the dream and everything to do with Grace.

On an oath he dragged her to him and covered her mouth with his.

Six

He'd kissed her before, so it wasn't the fierce, sudden rush of heat that shocked Grace. He'd held her in his arms before, so it wasn't the exhilaration of his muscled body pressed against hers that shocked her, either.

What shocked Grace was the *intensity* of the pleasure racing through her blood. The savage, hungry desire that had sprung to life at the first touch of his mouth on hers.

She'd never experienced such need before, would never have believed such depth of feeling even existed. Still wasn't certain that *she* wasn't the one having the dream instead of Rand.

But if this were a dream, she thought dimly, she didn't want to ever wake up.

His mouth moved over hers, deepened the kiss as his arms circled her shoulders and pulled her close.

On the edge of a cliff, only a fool does handstands.

The thought jumped into her dazed mind. Good heavens, she was not only doing handstands, she was doing cartwheels and flips. It would be a long fall over the edge of this cliff she stood on with Rand. A long, hard dive into certain heartache.

She was beyond caring. Beyond rational thought. She wanted this man like she'd never wanted before, and she was too far gone to stop what was happening. She didn't want to stop it.

He whispered her name between kisses, and the rough, husky sound of his voice made her pulse race even faster. His mouth, hot and demanding, slanted against hers again and again, the stubble of his beard sending sparks of electricity coursing through her veins. Grace opened to him, met the hungry thrust of his tongue with her own. She recognized the subtle taste of mint and the darker, more exotic taste of Rand himself. The masculine, earthy scent of his skin invaded her senses, heightened them, made her more aware of him and of the night surrounding them, the crescent moon overhead, the dim glow of the dying fire, the distant howl of a coyote.

The sensations all swirled upward in her mind and her body; they spun faster, and faster still. She wound her arms tightly around his shoulders and held on, let herself be drawn upward and carried away with the tornado of feelings he evoked in her.

From the first moment she'd seen him working in

the barn, she'd known it would be like this. Not in her head, she couldn't have imagined anything this intense. But in her heart, in her soul, she had known. She'd tried to tell herself she could manage her feelings for Rand, the physical and the professional. But she'd been wrong. So very wrong.

She'd seen something, felt something, the instant their eyes had met that first time. Something that went beyond understanding or explanation, and certainly beyond common sense.

His hands tightened on her shoulders, then he lifted his mouth from hers and looked down at her.

"Grace," he said raggedly, "if you want to stop this, you need to say so right now."

He offered no tender words, no soft whispers of endearment. What he did offer, Grace understood, was honesty. No lies, no promises. Nothing beyond this moment.

Was that enough for her? she asked herself. Could she make love with this man, knowing that this was all there was?

She looked into his dark eyes, saw an edge she'd never seen before, the same edge she heard in his voice. It was raw and primal, filled with need.

He frightened her.

He thrilled her.

Grace had waited all her life for this. For him.

She might be a fool, but her heart and her body simply wouldn't listen to her head. Lifting her hand to his cheek, she lightly traced the firm line of his mouth with her thumb. She felt a muscle jump in his jaw at her touch, watched those dark eyes of his narrow with passion.

"Make love to me, Rand," she whispered. "Please make love to me."

She was certain she saw relief in his eyes, then he caught her to him again and crushed his mouth to hers. She felt and tasted his desperation in the long, searing kiss he gave her.

Then he let her go.

Confused, she watched as he shoved the sleeping bag off him and rose.

"What—"

He bent down and kissed her again, a quick, heated brush of lips. "I'll be right back."

It took a moment for Grace to comprehend what Rand was doing, but when he walked to the cab of his truck and rifled through the glove box, she understood. She felt her cheeks warm with embarrassment. She'd been so completely lost in his touch, she hadn't thought about protection.

He kept his gaze on her as he walked back toward her. The pale light of the dying flames cast shadows over the hard, sharp angles of his face. His eyes narrowed with need.

She shivered.

When he knelt in front of her, she rose on her knees to face him. Slowly, hesitantly, Grace lifted her hand and laid it on his chest. She felt the wild beating of his heart under her palm and the heat of his skin through the light flannel shirt he wore.

Like an electrical current, desire vibrated from his

body to hers, then back again. When he covered her hand with his own, the voltage only increased.

"Grace," he said her name with velvet softness, "I don't want to hurt you. You need to be sure about this."

Didn't he know they were way beyond that? That the hurt was inevitable, and still she wanted him, wanted this, more than her next breath?

That wasn't something she could tell him.

But she could show him.

Grace laid her other hand on Rand's broad chest and splayed her fingers, moved upward, over his collarbone, felt the tension radiate from his body. She moved her fingers up his neck, then cupped his face in both of her hands. Her gaze held steady with his.

"Kiss me," she whispered.

His eyes narrowed with need, then he lowered his head to hers and captured her mouth. His kiss was gentle, yet insistent. His tongue lightly brushed over her bottom lip, then parted her lips and moved inside. She opened to him, welcomed him, and together they moved in a steady, primitive rhythm as old as time.

The kiss deepened. Grace felt her pulse pounding in her head, in her veins. She'd never felt so alive, so sensitive to every touch, every sound, every smell.

He pulled her tightly into his arms, held her close to the solid heat of his body. She shuddered. When his head dipped lower and blazed a hot trail of kisses down to the rise of her breast, she moaned.

"I want to see you," he said huskily, then slipped his hands under her T-shirt.

Grace sucked in a breath at the first glorious touch of his fingers on her bare skin. His rough, callused palms skimmed up the sides of her waist. Ripples of heat coursed through her body. She wanted those hands everywhere. Wanted her hands on him.

Breathing hard, she inched away from him, held his gaze with her own as she reached for the hem of her T-shirt and pulled it over her head.

She tossed it aside, and was naked from the waist up.

Rand's gaze dropped to her breasts; his eyes turned black as the night surrounding them, burned hot as the embers in the fire.

His hands slid upward.

She trembled at his touch. When his hands cupped her, she drew in a quick breath. Grace felt her skin tighten, felt the hot rush of blood pumping through her veins. Certain she would fall if she didn't hold on to him, she slid her hands up his forearms, felt the light sprinkling of coarse hair and the ripple of hard muscles.

"You're so damn beautiful," he murmured.

His thumbs brushed over her hardened nipples. Arrows of white-hot pleasure shot directly from her breasts to the juncture of her thighs. On a soft moan she closed her eyes and dropped her head back.

Nothing had ever felt so right to her before, so completely natural, and because of that, Grace felt no embarrassment or awkwardness. She simply let herself *feel,* and the sensations engulfed her. She wouldn't have believed it possible to experience pleasure this intense.

And then he bent and took her in his mouth.

Grace gasped at the feel of his tongue on her beaded nipple and the rasp of his beard on her soft flesh. She gripped his head in her hands and raked her fingers through his thick hair, struggled to drag oxygen into her lungs. Her heart slammed in her chest as he moved his hot, wet tongue in a sensual, rhythmic movement, then lightly scraped her sensitive skin with his teeth. Shock waves rippled through her, an electrifying, glorious raging river of need.

She hadn't had time to draw in a breath before he moved to her other breast and once again hungrily pulled her into his mouth. Pleasure bordered on pain. A steady, insistent throb pulsed between her legs. If it were possible to die from feelings this intense, then she was certain she would.

"Your clothes," she gasped between breaths and moved her hands restlessly over his shoulders. "I want to touch you."

He pulled away from her, his breathing ragged and heavy, then tore at the buttons on his shirt and yanked it off his shoulders. The firelight danced over his bronze skin and rippling muscles. He was the most magnificent man she'd ever seen: his shoulders were broad, his chest wide, his belly flat and hard. It was a warrior's body, marked with the scars of his battles. She laid her palms on his chest and splayed her hands, then lightly traced his flat, tiny nipples with the tips of her index fingers. He jumped at her touch, and she felt his shudder vibrate from his body to hers.

He caught her in his arms and his mouth swooped down on hers again, pulling her in, tasting, taking. Destroying. He demanded more, and she gave him everything. Bare flesh to bare flesh. She wrapped her arms around his shoulders and held on. Even as they fell backward on the thick sleeping bags, his mouth never left hers. Rand's long, muscled body pressed down on her, and she reveled in the feel of his weight on top of her. She wanted him closer still, and she hugged him tightly to her, moving her hips against him in a slow, sensual motion.

From deep in Rand's throat, Grace heard a rough sound, half growl, half moan. He grasped her hips with his large hands and held her still, then blazed hot kisses over her jaw and down her neck. Grace sucked in breath after breath with every nip of his teeth and sweep of his moist tongue. It seemed as if she'd been turned inside out, exposing every raw nerve to his touch. He moved down, over her shoulders, the swell of her breast, pausing to once again take each aching nipple into his mouth before moving lower still. His beard scraped at the soft skin on her belly; his tongue tasted hungrily.

He opened the snap of her jeans, and she heard the hiss of her zipper as the snug denim parted. While his mouth explored the valley of her hip, he eased the garment down inch by agonizing inch. When he nipped at the soft cotton-encased mound of her womanhood, Grace heard the sound of her moan. Gasping, her hands reached for his head, and she clawed her fingers into his hair.

It felt like a lifetime before her legs were finally free of her jeans. He linked two fingers under the elastic band of her underwear and in one swift, smooth move, they were gone, as well.

She lay naked under him, physically and emotionally, but it felt as natural to her as breathing.

He rose over her, his eyes intent and glinting with passion. He kept that dark gaze on her when he reached for the button on his jeans. Her chest rose and fell as she watched him slide open the zipper, then push denim down, moving away only momentarily to shrug the garment off. He stared down at her, the look in his eyes primal and possessive.

''Rand,'' she said his name on a ragged whisper and held her hand out to him. Flames from the fire reflected in his narrowed eyes.

Rand reached out and took her hand, linked his fingers with hers. He'd never seen anything more beautiful than Grace. Her hair fanned around her flushed face; sparks of red and gold danced in the wavy mass of shiny strands. Her lips were swollen from his kisses and softly parted, her eyes deep, deep green, glazed with desire. Her breasts were full, the tight buds of her velvet-soft nipples rosy. Her skin was like porcelain, a sharp contrast against his own.

He felt a need he'd never experienced with such intensity before, and the realiᴢation startled him. He quite simply had to have her or die.

His name was still on her lips as she pulled him

toward her. He took her other hand and linked their fingers, then lifted her arms over her head as he moved between her legs. He entered her slowly, watched her draw in a quick breath at the initial invasion, then closed her eyes on a soft moan.

"Open your eyes, Grace," he murmured. "Look at me."

Her eyes drifted open again, and she met his gaze. He brought his mouth to hers, brushed her lips with his, then began to move. When she sucked in another sharp breath and tightened her body, he stopped abruptly and lifted his head to frown down at her.

"What…?"

"Don't stop, Rand," she gasped. "Please don't stop."

With her legs wrapped tightly around him, Rand was finding it difficult to think. "Grace, I…wait…"

She shook her head, then surged upward, taking him deep inside her. She was so tight, so ready for him, and it was impossible not to move. Sweat beaded on his forehead; her fingers tightened in his. His entire body throbbed with need, a fierce pounding in his veins and his head that demanded release.

He moved faster, sheathed himself deeper still and she took him in, met him thrust for thrust, moan for moan. He felt her shudder under him, felt her inner muscles tighten and clench as she arched upward sharply on a cry. The shudder rolled from her body to his, intensified until he could hold back no longer. With a guttural cry, he drove into her. The climax shattered wildly out of control, as wild and primitive as the night surrounding them.

Her name on his lips, he gathered her in his arms and waited for his world to steady again.

Grace felt as if she were drifting, as if the breeze had swept her up and carried her away. Her head rested on Rand's chest and she heard the still, heavy beating of his heart, felt his chest rise and fall with each breath. She'd never known such contentment, such bliss, and to think that she'd found it here, in Rand's arms, on the edge of a steep canyon, seemed fitting.

"Grace." He said her name softly as he tucked a wayward strand of hair behind her ear. "Why didn't you tell me?"

She rose on one elbow and glanced down at him. He looked much too serious, she thought. "Tell you what?" she teased.

He frowned at her. "You know what."

She lifted a shoulder, then traced circles on his chest with the tip of her finger. "You mean that I was... inexperienced?"

"I made an assumption that you'd probably done this before."

"Well, that's what you get for making assumptions," she said, and nestled back into his arms. "And I'm in too good a mood to argue about it. If you have a problem with it, then it's your problem."

He rolled her onto her back, his eyes narrowed as he gazed down at her. "Did I say I had a problem?

I'm just a little...surprised. You're twenty-five years old.''

She rolled her eyes. ''You're making me sound like an old maid, for heaven's sake. Just because I waited a little longer than most women, doesn't mean I qualify for senior citizenship.''

He stroked a hand over her shoulder and down her arm, his expression thoughtful. ''So why have you waited?''

She shrugged, feeling a little foolish now. ''It just never seemed quite right to me before, that's all. That might sound old-fashioned to most people, but I wanted my first time to be special.'' She reached up and touched his cheek. ''You made it special for me. Thank you.''

Grace felt Rand stiffen, saw the mixture of uncertainty and hesitation in his eyes. She understood that what had just happened between them might not be special to Rand, that he'd been with lots of women before.

The thought felt like a knife in her heart, but she refused to let him see the hurt, and she also refused to let him spoil the moment.

She dropped her hand from his face and frowned at him. ''Rand Sloan, whatever you're thinking, stop it right now. I'm a big girl. I'm not asking or expecting anything from you, so stop looking as if I just locked the barn door behind you.''

He stared at her for a long moment, then sat and raked his hands through his hair. Certain that he was already turning away from her, Grace felt her throat thicken. She wouldn't cry, dammit. She wouldn't.

"Blackhawk."

She looked at his stiff back, not certain she'd heard him right. "What?"

"My real name is Rand Jedidiah Blackhawk," he said quietly. "My parents were Jonathan and Norah Blackhawk of Wolf River."

Blackhawk. The name was so familiar to Grace, but she couldn't place it at the moment. She pulled the sleeping bag up to cover her bare torso, then sat slowly.

"My brother was Seth Ezekiel Blackhawk," Rand went on. "My sister, Elizabeth Marie."

He had a sister and brother? She felt the tension radiate from him but said nothing, just waited for him to continue.

"I'd been told that they died in the accident that killed my parents." He stared into the darkness, his gaze fixed but unseeing. "Seth was seven, Lizzie was barely three."

"Are you saying they weren't killed?" she asked incredulously.

"Three days ago I received a letter from a lawyer in Wolf River telling me that they're alive," he said tightly. "Twenty-three years and all this time they've been alive, living somewhere else, like I was, with other families."

Grace understood now why Rand's mother had asked her if she were a lawyer and told her that she'd better give Rand a wide berth if she were. She could only imagine his shock at learning the sister and brother he'd thought dead were alive. "Who would do such a horrible thing?" she asked. "And why?"

"My uncle was filled with hate," Rand said. "I saw it in his eyes that night when he handed me over to that woman. He wouldn't have wanted his brother's half-breed children near one penny of whatever small estate my parents had, and he certainly wouldn't have raised us himself. So he farmed us out, sold us to the highest bidders and made sure each of us thought the other was dead so he'd never have to deal with any of us again."

Appalled, Grace sucked in a slow breath and tried to absorb what Rand was telling her. Three small children had not only lost their parents, they'd been separated and told the others were dead, too. The injustice of it all sickened her.

"When I find my uncle," Rand said coldly, "I'll kill him with my bare hands."

Rand turned and looked at her, and Grace shivered under the murderous glint in his eyes. It frightened her that he just might follow through on his threat. While she couldn't blame him, Grace knew that no good would come of it. He stiffened when she laid her cheek on his shoulder, but he did not pull away.

"Your nightmare," she said softly. "Was that what you were dreaming about? The accident and your family?"

He nodded. "We were all coming back from town and got caught in a summer storm. A lightning bolt struck the road in front of our car and my dad lost control. We rolled over and went into a ravine." He closed his eyes. "My memory is spotty after that. I was cold and wet. There was blood on my shirt and pants. The sheriff pulled me out of the car, and my uncle was there with a woman. He never even spoke to me, just told the woman to take me away."

"Who was she?"

"I don't know. But she was the one who told me my family had died, that I had to go live somewhere else." He stared at the red-glowing embers of the fire. "I wanted to die, too. I was angry that I hadn't."

Rand's voice was so distant that Grace realized he truly wasn't speaking to her. The muscles across his back and shoulders were tight, his jaw clenched. She pictured him as a frightened child, alone and hurt, without his family, and she had a sudden, fierce desire to seek retribution on that horrible, horrible man who'd done this to him.

She steadied her own emotions, and gently stroked his arm and back. Slowly she felt him relax and lean into her. "What are you going to do now?"

He shook his head and sighed deeply. "It's been twenty-three years, Grace. Seth and Lizzie may not even remember me. They have their own lives now and I wouldn't want to disrupt that. I don't see where I can fit in."

That had always been his problem, Grace realized. That after losing his family, he'd simply never fit in anywhere. He'd drifted from town to town, ranch to ranch. Never stayed in one place. Survivor's guilt, she'd heard it called. He'd never felt that he deserved a real home, or even love, for himself.

"But what if they do remember you?" she asked him. "What if all these years they've missed you, dreamed about you, too? You were their big brother, Rand. How could they forget you? Once they know you're not dead, they'll want you to be in their lives."

"Maybe." He sucked in a long breath and let it out. "Maybe not. Hey, what's this?"

He glanced down at her, at the tears that spilled from her eyes onto his arm. He turned and wiped at her eyes with his thumb. "Tears for me, Grace?" he said solemnly.

She shook her head. "For a nine-year-old boy who lost his family."

He smiled softly and gathered her in his arms. "Thank you," he said softly, tipped her face to his and kissed her tears, then brought his mouth to hers.

Grace tasted the salt of her own tears on his lips, the sadness, then, as the kiss deepened, the growing desire. When he pulled her into his lap, she slid her arms around his shoulders, wanting to give him so much more than her body. But as his kiss deepened, her body deceived her. The urgency to be close with him again, to make love with him and hold him inside her body, coiled tightly inside her. They were both breathing hard, their hearts beating wildly as he laid her back on the sleeping bag.

"Grace," he said on a ragged whisper, "I don't want to hurt you."

Did he mean physically, she wondered, or emotionally? Either way, it was too late, she knew. She answered him by dragging his mouth back to hers and arching her body upward to meet his. When he slid inside her, she nearly sobbed with the joy of the moment. There was no pain, only pleasure. Sweet pleasure that grew stronger with every thrust, with every kiss, with every whisper. For this moment he was hers, as she was his.

She held on to him; he held on to her, both of them driving toward that blissful end with a desperation that staggered the senses. When it came, they tumbled breathlessly, hopelessly, over that steep, jagged cliff together.

Grace woke early the next morning to the song of birds, a cool breeze on her face and the smell of a campfire. She was alone in her sleeping bag, but she could hear Rand close by, talking to the horses. She'd pulled her clothes on before they'd finally gone to sleep a few hours ago, and she snuggled in the warmth of her covers for a moment, letting herself enjoy the memories of the night before. A smile slowly spread on her face.

Rand had been a wonderful, exciting lover, and Grace knew she would always cherish the night they'd spent together. She'd be a fool to think that their relationship would ever be more, but she'd already been a fool once, so she couldn't stop herself from hoping. Wisdom and intellect seemed to take a back seat to matters of the heart.

She rose on one elbow, then stretched. She was

sore, but not overly so considering the night she'd had. She glanced at Rand, watched him lead the horses back from the creek where he'd taken them to drink the cool water. He wore a chambray shirt today and a pair of faded jeans. His dark hair was mussed, his beard more than a stubble. She could picture him with a star on his shirt, a Western marshall, on the hunt for escaped bank robbers.

The wave of desire that shivered up her spine startled her. Already she wanted him again, wanted her hands and mouth on him and his on her. When he glanced at her, leveled those black eyes on her, her breath caught.

Her heart pounded furiously when he dropped the horses' reins and started toward her. She felt her blood race through her veins.

The crackle of the two-way radio inside his truck stopped him. She saw the regret when he changed direction and walked toward his truck to answer the call. He kept his back to her as he talked, and when he turned to face her, his expression was somber.

"What is it?" she asked, already afraid of his answer.

"There's a storm on the way," he said, keeping his gaze on her. "We have to go back."

Seven

"Go back?" Grace repeated. "You mean leave?"

"That was your brother on the radio," Rand said evenly. "He and Marty are stuck in a thunderstorm at the base camp."

The rosy blush that had been on Grace's cheeks only a moment ago vanished. Her face turned pale as she stared at him. "Are they all right?"

"Everyone's fine, but the storm has them penned in for now. They have no idea when they can get out."

She was already out of her sleeping bag and tugging her boots on. "So we'll go without them."

"Like hell we will. Even if we find those horses, and that's a big *if*, darlin', you haven't got the strength or the experience to bring them in."

"I'm stronger than I look, Rand," she said, pulling

her jeans down over her boots. "And I'm a fast learner."

She stood and closed the top button on her jeans, but not before he caught a flash of her flat belly. His heart slammed in his chest, remembering how he'd slid his hand over and kissed that smooth, soft skin. He was hard instantly, wanting her again with the same urgency as the night before. She was a fast learner, all right, he thought as he recalled how she'd felt in his arms and the way she'd brought him to a fever pitch.

It took a will of iron to force his thoughts back to their conversation. "Dammit, Grace, this isn't a Sunday ride in the park. This could be dangerous. You could get hurt, and if that storm does come in while we're in the canyon, you could even get dead."

"We can do this, Rand. I know we can." She reached for the blue denim shirt she'd laid out on a rock the night before, shook it vigorously, then pulled it on over the T-shirt she wore. "There's not a cloud in the sky. We don't know the storm will come this way."

"We don't know that it won't."

"I swear to you," she pleaded, "if it starts to look risky, I'll turn back without an argument."

He shook his head. "We're not going."

She moved toward him, those long legs of hers encased in snug denim, and his pulse jumped. He clenched his jaw, refusing to let her see how strongly she affected him. How badly he wanted her. No woman had ever had that kind of power over him before, and he was determined no woman ever would.

"I mean it, Grace." He folded his arms, steeled himself against the look of determination in her eyes.

"We've come all this way, Rand," she said softly, and slid her arms around his neck. "We can't turn back now."

Damn her, anyway, Rand thought irritably. She wasn't playing fair at all, here. "Grace—"

She silenced him with her lips, and he felt the last of his resistance melt away.

Dammit, dammit, dammit.

"Please, Rand," she begged him. "I promise I'll do exactly what you say. We can't just leave them there to die."

She was right, dammit. In spite of everything he'd said, he knew she was right. He couldn't leave them. Not without trying.

On an oath, he took her arms and pulled them away from him. He felt a muscle jump in his temple as he stared down at her. "Be ready in two minutes or I'll leave without you. If we haven't found them within an hour, or at the first sign of bad weather, we're coming back. If you argue, I swear I'll dress you up like a Thanksgiving turkey and you'll ride back on your stomach instead of your butt. You got that?"

She nodded, a smile on her lips, but an edge of fear in her eyes, too. Good, he thought. He needed her to be afraid. It would keep her alert and focused and ready to move quickly.

He released her and turned on his heel. While he

saddled the horses, he alternately cursed her and himself. He was a damn fool, he knew, but he couldn't refuse her. She could have asked him to take down a charging bull with his bare hands and he would have done it.

She'd gotten to him, he realized with dread, and resolved that by the time this day had ended, he'd be back in control and Miss Grace Sullivan would be on her way home where she belonged.

It took them thirty minutes to get down the steep path to the bottom of the canyon. Dawn crept over the high cliffs in ribbons of pink and blue while a pair of hawks circled overhead and desert cottontails darted in and out of low-lying shrubs of mesquite and cottonwood. Rand searched the sky for any sign of clouds moving in. So far, so good, he thought with a sigh of relief.

Now if only they could find the horses that smoothly.

They hadn't spoken on the ride down, and he was thankful for that. He was still reeling, still unbalanced from the night they'd spent together, and he had no idea what to say to her. *Thanks Grace for letting me be your first, and see you around.*

How could he have known she was a virgin? She was a grown woman, for crying out loud. It had never entered his mind that she hadn't been with a man before.

But she hadn't. And though he wasn't proud of it, there was a part of him, that primitive male arrogance, that was actually glad he was her first. She'd said he'd made it special for her, but she'd made it special for him, too. Special in a way it never had been before.

He'd always been careful when it came to sex. Not only for health reasons, but he'd never wanted to worry that he'd left a woman pregnant behind him. The thought of a child—his child—without a father, was unthinkable for him. If he had gotten a woman pregnant, he would have had to settle down, get married, even. He never would have let any kid of his grow up without a father or be raised by another man. There were too many Edward Sloans in the world, and the thought of his own son or daughter living under that kind of harsh control made his chest tighten.

And what kind of father would he make, anyway? Rand thought. What did he know about babies and cuddling and bottles? Babies terrified him. They were so tiny and helpless. He'd rather bare-hand a rattlesnake than change a diaper.

He glanced over his shoulder at Grace when they were on level ground again. She rode maybe fifteen feet behind him on the pinto mare and had managed to keep up with him all the way down the trail, even when it had narrowed and grown steeper. She did know how to ride; he'd give her that much. She looked comfortable in the saddle, completely at ease. The white Stetson she wore was a sharp contrast to her dark, auburn curls. Her cheeks were flushed, her deep-green eyes alert and sparkling.

Something slammed in Rand's chest. Lust, most definitely. But something more than that. Something that made him sweat.

There was no future for them, he was certain of that. But that didn't stop him from wanting her.

He tore his gaze from her, then reined his own horse in and studied the canyon while he waited for Grace to catch up with him. The canyon narrowed behind them, so the horses had to be ahead. The map he'd studied had shown the canyon to be only five miles long, with fairly steep cliffs on either side. The trail they'd just come down was the only way in and only way out. With enough time and a couple of extra hands, it wouldn't be that difficult to box the herd in and capture them. But they didn't have time or extra hands. Though he didn't see any clouds, he'd already felt a subtle change in the air, and he suspected the weather would not stay as nice as it was at the moment for very long.

"We're downwind," he told Grace when she reined in beside him. "That will be to our advantage if we find them."

"*When* we find them," Grace said with conviction. "I know they're here. I can feel it."

Rand nodded. "They at least were here. I've seen some signs of grazing and some dried horse manure."

"So what are we waiting for?" she said impatiently. "Let's go find them."

"Grace." He put a hand out to steady her horse, wondered why he was having a difficult time saying what needed to be said. "You need to understand. Between lack of food and water and predators, they might be dead."

Her lips pressed into a thin line, and she shook her head. "I refuse to believe that."

"You have to prepare yourself," he said. "You have to be ready to accept whatever you find. And you have to accept what I'll need to do if they're sick or not strong enough to make the trip back out."

Grace glanced at the rifle he carried in a saddle holster. She sucked in a sharp breath and nodded. "I know."

They rode in silence for the next few minutes, with Grace close behind. Rand knew she was thinking about what he'd said. She was worried about what he might have to do if the animals were too far gone to help. That part of his work had always been the most difficult, and he didn't want to dwell on the possibility right now. But the canyon appeared dry, and unless the horses had found water somewhere, they would most certainly be a lost cause.

The world is full of lost causes, Mary had said to him in the barn the night before he'd left. *Those are the ones who need help the most.*

His mother had known that he needed to take this trip not just for the horses, but for himself. He wasn't so dense as to not see the correlation between his own life and a lost band of horses, but he was a grown man. He had control of his life, he understood where he came from and accepted it. He'd never felt sorry for himself and he sure as hell didn't want anyone else to, either.

And what about Seth and Lizzie? What had their lives been like? Where did they live? Were they married, with a dozen kids between them? Did he have nieces and nephews? The thought made his chest ache, made him wonder things he'd hadn't truly allowed himself to wonder since he'd received that letter. And from that wonder came something else he'd never allowed himself before. Something he'd shut off the night that woman had taken him away.

Hope.

Grace had told him that his sister and brother could never forget him, not completely. Could she be right? Even if they thought he'd been killed, as he'd thought they had, did they still have memories? Would they welcome him into their lives? Or would they blame him? He was the oldest, he should have taken care of them, protected them.

The sudden splatter of raindrops on his hands brought Rand to a halt. Dammit! He'd been so lost in thought that he hadn't noticed how quickly the dark clouds were rolling in. He jerked his gaze to the sky and swore again, then turned to look at Grace.

"We're going to have to turn back."

The misery on her face said it all, but true to her promise to him, she didn't argue. Her shoulders slumped in defeat, and she nodded weakly.

He turned his mount, then froze at the sound of a high-pitched whinny. Grace's horse whinnied in response and stamped its front hooves. Eyes wide, Grace snapped her gaze to his.

"Rand," she said his name on a breathless whisper.

"I'll be a son of a gun," he muttered out loud. They'd found them! They'd actually found them!

The rain started to come down harder, and the large drops bounced off the dry canyon floor and began to puddle in the dusty dirt.

Grace looked at him, her expression anxious. She'd do whatever he said, Rand knew, even if it meant turning around now. He heard another distant whinny, and gauged the sound to be just around an outcropping of rocks no more than an hundred yards away.

And then he knew that there really was no decision. That probably there never really had been. Come hell or high water—and he hoped like hell there'd be no high water—he knew he couldn't turn back now.

"We won't have much time," he said roughly, keeping his voice low. "We're going to need the element of surprise. If the lead horse catches wind of us, he'll take off for the deep end of the canyon and we won't stand a chance."

"What should I do?" she asked.

"Stay here and be ready." He reached for the rope looped around the back of his saddle. "If I can get close enough to a mare and get hold of her, our only chance is that the stallion will follow, and the rest of the horses will follow him. It's a long shot, but it's all we've got."

He leaned over and reached for Grace, surprising her and himself both when he kissed her hard and quick. "For luck," he said, then took off at a gallop.

Stunned, Grace watched him ride off, her heart racing as he disappeared around the rocks. She pressed her fingertips to her mouth, her lips still tingling from his kiss. She barely noticed the rain coming down steadily now.

He'd gone after them, she thought, and the excitement and the thrill of it shimmered over her now wet skin. After all he'd said, he'd still gone after them. He wasn't as hard-hearted or as practical or logical as he wanted everyone to believe. She'd seen the look in his eyes when they'd turned to start back. He'd been just as upset as she had been, just as devastated.

She still wasn't completely clear what his plan was, but he'd told her to be ready, whatever that meant, so she kept her gaze on the spot where he'd vanished, listening, waiting.

But for what?

The rain fell harder still, and the distant sound of thunder had her horse prancing nervously under her. Grace kept a firm hold on the reins and her knees tight against her horse. The minutes ticked by, though it felt like hours. Rain poured off the brim of her hat, and she watched nervously as the water in the canyon began to rise and flow in the direction Rand had ridden.

Rand, she said a silent prayer that he was all right. *Hurry, please, hurry.*

The thought of anything happening to him terrified her. She told herself not to worry, that he was experienced and he knew what he was doing. But anything could go wrong, one wrong move and he could be lying with a broken leg or unconscious. The image made the knots in her stomach tighten.

He was all right, she told herself. He *had* to be.

She loved him.

God help her, but she knew that without a doubt now. She cursed herself for not telling him how she felt. He didn't have to love her back. She just wanted him to know, needed him to know.

She gripped the reins so tightly in her hand that the leather cut into her palm. "Where *are* you, dammit?" she said out loud.

As if he'd heard her, Rand came barreling around the rocks, splashing through the slowly rising river of water. A small bay mare, eyes wide with fear and confusion, galloped beside him. A rope around her neck kept her tied to Rand's saddle.

And chasing behind them, his proud neck held high and his mane waving, came the stallion. The animal was larger than most wild stallions, his coat pitch-black. He looked thin, but not emaciated. If it were possible to read an expression in the animal's eyes, Grace would have said that he was furious at the mare's capture and he intended to get her back. Behind the stallion came three more mares... and two foals!

Rand said nothing, just waved at Grace, signaled for her to get behind the small herd and follow. She swung her horse around and dropped in back of the animals. So intent was the herd on keeping up with the stallion, they didn't seem to notice her.

The group moved as one, the natural instinct of horses to stay with the herd keeping them all close together. The sky had opened up by the time Rand reached the spot where they'd come down. The ground was turning to mud, and Grace knew they'd have to get up the trail quickly, or they all would be in danger of slipping over the edges where it narrowed.

Rand went up first, dragging the mare he'd roped behind him. The horse balked when she first hit the trail, then followed. The stallion whinnied loudly and reared, then he followed, too, as did the other mares. It took every ounce of strength Grace had to keep her horse heading upward after the other horses. Her leg muscles screamed in protest, but she knew she had to hold tight in the saddle or she'd fall off for certain. Ahead of her, she watched Rand labor not only with his own horse, but the mare he pulled behind him. All of the horses pawed and struggled to get a footing in the mud and to keep together.

It was slow and dangerous, but they climbed upward, inch by inch, foot by foot, horse and humans together. The smell of wet leather and horse assailed Grace's senses; rain slapped at her face and poured off her hat. Eyes wide with determination, his nostrils flared, the stallion kept up with Rand's horse and the mare that had been stolen from him.

One of the foals slipped at the narrowest passage and its hind leg went out from under him. Grace bit her lip to keep from screaming as she watched the terrified animal slide over the edge, then catch its footing at the last minute and scramble back up with its mother.

Thunder rumbled, and the storm pounded at them. Grace made the mistake of glancing back down into the canyon, and the sight of the rising, rushing water nearly paralyzed her. Ten minutes more down there and they all would have been swept away. Clenching her jaw, she turned her attention back to the trail and what lay ahead, not behind her.

The rain blinded her, but her hat kept the worst of it off her face. She lost track of time, concentrating solely on staying in the saddle and keeping her horse on the disappearing trail. Rocks and mud slid down the trail and more than once the horse she rode stumbled, then gained her footing again.

When at last they hit the top, Grace slumped in her saddle, so exhausted she wasn't certain she could ride another foot. She let her horse take over now and carry her back to their camp. The herd followed the captured mare and Grace could do little more than watch as Rand quickly slid off his horse and roped the stallion, then tied him to a tree.

She knew better than to call to Rand or try to catch his attention. The wild horses weren't used to humans and their presence would frighten them. She closed her eyes and said a silent prayer of thanks, holding tightly to her saddle horn for fear she might fall off her mount. She barely noticed the rain anymore, she was already as wet as she could get, so it hardly mattered.

Her eyes flew open at Rand's touch on her leg. He reached up for her, and she slid off her horse into his arms.

"You did it, you did it," she said over and over and threw her arms around his shoulders.

Smiling, he lifted her up off the ground and hugged her tightly. "*We* did it," he said.

"Oh, Rand." Grace began to laugh. "I love you."

He stilled at her words, and she knew instantly that she'd made a mistake. But she didn't care. She *did* love him, and he was just going to have to deal with it. Or not. Whichever, the decision was his.

But she was too happy right now to let her slip of the tongue ruin this wonderful moment. She hugged him tightly, and the exhaustion she'd felt only a moment ago vanished. She felt like Gene Kelly at the moment—she could dance and sing in the rain and splash in the puddles and not give two hoots that she was soaked to the bone.

Rand carried her to the truck, then opened the door and set her inside. ''I've got to get our saddles off our horses,'' he said, and closed the door behind her.

Grace felt useless, and she would have gone to help him, but she knew that he could do it faster than she could, anyway, and she would only be in the way. She felt an ache in her chest at the thought, knowing that was probably how he viewed her intrusion into his life, as someone who would only be in his way.

So here she was, head over heels for the first time in her life, and after today she would probably never see him again. Her throat thickened and her eyes burned, but she blinked back her tears. She was celebrating today, dammit! She would deal with the hurt and the pain later. Right now she was determined to enjoy the success of rounding up the strays.

Rand jumped into the truck a minute later, whipped his hat off and tossed it onto the back seat of the dual cab. Grace sat huddled against the door, her hair dripping, her clothes drenched.

"Are they all right?" she asked, and realized her teeth were chattering.

He nodded, then looked at her in dismay. "God, you're soaking wet."

She had no idea why she found that funny. Perhaps it was his astute observation of the obvious, or the fact that he was just as wet as she was, but she started laughing. He looked at her as if she'd gone crazy. A smile tugged at the corner of his mouth and spread, and then he was laughing, too.

It was the first time she'd really heard him laugh, and the sound made her forget everything—that they could have died or been seriously hurt, that she'd told him she loved him. Even that she was wet and cold and her legs ached.

Still laughing, he reached for her, pulled her into his arms and hugged her. "Ah, Grace," he said, shaking his head. "What in the world am I going to do with you?"

She felt the heat rise from his skin, the hard play of muscle under her body as he held her close. A smile touched her lips as she lifted her face to his.

"Anything you want, Rand Blackhawk Sloan," she murmured. "Everything you want."

Eight

Grace's words sucked the air from Rand's lungs and sent heat flooding through his body. In that instant he wanted her with an intensity that shocked him. It didn't matter that they were both soaking wet, or that they'd both come close to dying down in that canyon. If anything, those things heightened his awareness of her and the need clawing at his insides.

He crushed his mouth to hers, tasted the rain and the passion on her. She parted her lips for him; he dived inside. Eagerly, she met the insistent rhythm of his tongue with demands of her own. Never before had the hunger been so keen or so sharp. It staggered his senses, blinded him from everything and everyone else but the woman in his arms.

He had to have her. Had to make her his, even if it were only for this moment.

With his mouth still on hers, he scooted to the center of the truck and pulled her on top of him. She pulled back from him, her chest rising and falling rapidly. Her T-shirt and bra were plastered to her skin, and he could clearly see the outline of her breasts and hard nipples through the wet fabric. His heart hammered in his chest.

On an oath, he clamped his mouth to her breast through the fabric while he kneaded the soft flesh with his hands. She raked her hands through his wet hair and dragged him closer to her.

"Take this off," he demanded and tugged her T-shirt upward. She peeled the wet garment off, and once again he brought his mouth to her breast, sucking the nipple through the thin cotton of her bra. Gasping, she let her head fall forward.

He found the front clasp of her bra and unsnapped it. Her skin was cool and damp, and he could smell and taste the storm still on her. He took her breasts in his hands and his mouth, wanting desperately to kiss and touch her everywhere at once. She writhed over him, moving her body against him until he thought he might go mad with the need pulsing white-hot through his veins.

He unsnapped the button of her jeans and pulled the zipper down. She brought her mouth to his and kissed him while he slid his hands between denim and skin and eased the wet jeans down her hips. They struggled together to free her feet of boots and her legs from her pants, but then she was naked on top of him, reaching for him. He lifted his hips as she tugged his jeans free, but they made it no farther than his knees before she straddled him and he slid inside her.

They both groaned.

And then she began to move, and he groaned again.

He gripped her bottom in his hands and guided her as she moved up and down, each time driving him deeper inside her. Her nails bit into his shoulders, holding tightly as she drove them both closer to their destination.

Rain pounded the roof and thunder rumbled close by. But the real storm, the true storm, was here, inside this truck, in their need for each other.

"Rand," she gasped his name and her nails went deeper into his shoulders.

The climax hit them both with all the energy and intensity of a lightning bolt. She threw her head back and cried out. He groaned, a rough, hoarse sound that came from deep in his chest.

She sank forward, dragging in deep breaths while the tremors still rippled through her. His heart pounding furiously, his breathing ragged, he held her close and waited for the storm to ease.

Grace listened to the pattering of the rain on the roof of the truck. The sound soothed her, and with Rand's arms around her, their bodies still joined, she'd never known such contentment before.

"You all right?" He pressed a kiss to her temple and slid his hand up her back.

"Mmmm," was the best she could manage. She felt his smile against her cheek.

"I take it that means yes."

"Oh, yeah. And you?"

"Oh, yeah."

Now it was her turn to smile. She snuggled against him, enjoyed the gentle slide of his hand up and down her back. "We really need to get your clothes off."

He chuckled. "Damn, woman, give me a few minutes, will you?"

Grace felt her cheeks warm at his implication. "That's not what I meant. Your clothes are soaked and I just thought you'd want to change into something dry."

"I'll get out of them, all right," he murmured and smiled at her. "You're so damn cute when you blush."

She blushed deeper and ducked her head so he wouldn't see. He pulled her against him and tucked a long strand of wet hair behind her ear.

"Grace," he said, his tone suddenly somber.

Not now, she thought, closing her eyes. *Please not now.* If he gave her the lone-wolf, I'm not the type of guy to settle down speech, she didn't think she could stand it.

"You did good down there in the canyon."

She looked up at him, saw the sincerity in his eyes.

"Between the horses coming at you," he said, "the rising water, and getting back up that trail in the storm, it would have been easy to panic. You didn't."

"I was too scared to panic," she said truthfully.

"You're an amazing woman, Miss Grace Sullivan."

His compliment warmed her, though she truly didn't see where she'd done anything out of the ordinary.

"I was with you, Rand." She touched his lips with her fingertips. "I knew you could do it. That's why I wasn't afraid."

His eyes narrowed and darkened as he met her steady gaze, then he reached for her, dragged her mouth to his for a long, searing kiss that sent ribbons of heat curling all the way to her toes.

"How many minutes did you say you needed?" she asked in a ragged whisper.

He answered her question by sliding his hands to her hips and moving under her. Breathlessly she followed his lead, then took over until they were both clutching each other, both gasping, both shuddering.

I love you, Rand Blackhawk.

But this time she didn't say it out loud. She kept it to herself, praying, hoping that somewhere in his life and in his heart, he might find even the tiniest place for her.

They slept in the cab of the truck, in each other's arms, until the storm passed over. When they finally woke, Grace pulled on a fresh T-shirt and jeans and struggled to do something with her hair while Rand shucked his damp jeans and shirt and dragged on dry clothes. The sun was already starting to peek through the clouds when they stepped from the truck. The scent of damp earth filled the clean, fresh air.

The stallion reared at the sight of humans; his mares and foals whinnied and huddled nervously close by. Sidestepping and without making eye contact, Rand slowly approached the horses and tossed them an armful of alfalfa before he retreated again. They scattered and snorted, but the scent of the alfalfa won the animals over and soon they were all pushing and nipping at each other to gain access to the treat. When Rand carefully tossed two flakes of hay down, they scattered a second time, but eased back to the food once again and ate hungrily.

From a rock on the other side of the camp, Grace sat and watched the animals eat. The mares were roans, the foals, one bay and one chestnut. They were all thin, with patches of hair missing on their dull coats. The mares and foals had bite marks on them, the method by which the stallion kept his herd in line.

Wild mustangs were not the most attractive horses, but to Grace they were beautiful.

Rand came up behind her and slipped his arms around her. He smelled like hay and horses and man. She breathed in the scent of him and smiled.

"They would have died down there," she said quietly.

"They didn't," he said simply.

"Because of you."

"Not me, Grace. In case you've forgotten, I turned you down when you first asked me to come here with you. You were the one who never gave up, the one who really saved them, not me."

She didn't agree with him, but she didn't want to

argue, either. It was too perfect a day, too perfect a moment. She laid her head back against his chest and simply let herself enjoy their success.

"He's pretty bossy," Grace said, watching the stallion move between his mares and foals while he ate, nipping at them and pawing the ground.

"He just wants to make sure they stay close," Rand said. "He's stronger and smarter than they are. It's his job to protect them."

"Spoken like a true man," Grace teased. In the horse world, though, what Rand said was true. The lead stallion was the strongest and usually the smartest animal in his herd. Grace, however, did not believe that axiom transposed into the human world. She watched the stallion shake his mane and bare his teeth at one of the mares and was quite thankful that she was not a horse.

"The foals are pretty little things, aren't they?" Grace said absently. "We shouldn't have any trouble adopting them out."

She felt him stiffen. Furrowing her brow, she angled her head and glanced up at him. He stared at the horses, his lips hard and thin, the expression on his face solemn.

"Rand?"

He was silent for a moment, then sighed heavily. "I was just thinking about Lizzie. That it would have been the same for her. She was so beautiful. I can only imagine there would have been a long line of people wanting to adopt her."

It made sense that he would see the correlation between the wild horses and his siblings. And now, since he knew his sister and brother were alive, that he would wonder and worry what had happened to them.

"Who did she look like?" Grace asked, turning her gaze back to the horses.

"She had my mother's blue eyes," Rand said softly. "Her hair was lighter back then, not as dark as mine or Seth's. My mother used to say our sister had hair the same color as our Grandma Cordelia in Wales. Not a true black, but a deep, dark, sable brown. Even as a baby, Lizzie had an exotic look about her."

"She'll remember you, Rand," Grace said with resolution. "Maybe not as clearly as Seth will, but when she meets you, she'll know in her heart who you are."

When she meets you. Grace's words made Rand's heart slam in his chest. He hadn't made that decision yet, hadn't even allowed himself to think about it since he'd told Grace last night about Lizzie and Seth.

Grace stroked his forearm with the tips of her fingers, and Rand felt himself relax under her touch. She'd cried for him last night, he remembered. In his adult life, no woman had ever done that for him before. There'd been tears of anger, tears of frustration and tears intended to manipulate, but never tears for *him.*

And she'd told him that she loved him.

He knew that she'd said the words in a moment of exhilaration after they'd brought the horses up from the canyon. Had she truly meant them?

Of course she hadn't. She'd just been caught up in the moment, he told himself. Even if she did think she loved him, he didn't believe she really did, or that she could. They were too different, from two different worlds. In time those differences would overshadow any feelings she thought she might have for him.

He'd be leaving soon, going back to San Antonio, and she'd be going back to Dallas. But he knew he'd never forget her.

He pulled her to her feet, and she went into his arms. Tenderly he kissed her. "Thank you."

"For what?" she said, her voice soft and breathless.

"I wouldn't have come here if it hadn't been for you. Mary was right when she told me I needed to do some thinking. A place like this puts things in perspective."

"Does that mean you've made a decision about going to Wolf River?"

He nodded. "I'll stop there on my way back to San Antonio. At least listen to what that lawyer has to say."

"Oh, Rand." There were tears in her eyes when she cupped his face in her hands and kissed him. "I'm so glad."

But there was sadness in her eyes, as well. He saw it, knew she understood they would each be going their own way soon.

The realization at how close that time was hit him like a two-by-four. He dragged her against him and kissed her hard. She clung to him, kissing him back with the same desperation.

There was only one place for this kiss to lead, but

he didn't back away from it. He welcomed it, deepening the kiss as he lifted her and started for the truck.

They'd gone no more than a few feet when the sound of an engine reverberated off the rocks and shook the ground. Rand froze, then swore and set Grace back on the ground. The horses lifted their heads and pranced nervously.

The truck came into view a moment later. A large black truck pulling an eight-horse trailer.

With a groan Grace dropped her head onto Rand's shoulder.

"They're here," she said weakly, then stepped away from Rand and watched as her brother and another man drove up, then parked their rig and got out of the truck.

"I've never heard anything like it," Tom said, shaking his head in amazement after Grace told him how they'd brought the horses in by themselves. "I wanna hear this again, only this time slow down and give details."

Arms folded, Rand leaned back against his truck and listened while Grace told her brother and Marty, in detail, what had happened down in the canyon. Her elaborate and animated description of the mare's capture embarrassed Rand a little, but the light in her eyes and the smile on her lips was worth hearing her account, not once, but twice.

Tom appeared to be a likable enough guy. He was tall, probably around six-two. He had Grace's green eyes, but his hair was dark-brown instead of auburn, and he had a face that most women would take notice of. Rand had sensed some hostility in him when they'd first shaken hands, but that was certainly understandable. Rand knew that if Grace were his sister, and she'd just spent the past few days gallivanting around Texas with a stranger, he'd be hostile, too. No doubt that if Tom knew what else had gone on, he'd be a hell of a lot more than hostile.

There were some things that brothers were better off not knowing.

Rand rolled his eyes when Grace embellished her description of him as he'd come galloping around the rocks with the mare beside him and the stallion on his heels. The only things she left out were his eyes shooting lightning bolts and his mouth spitting flames.

With the extra hands and equipment the men had brought, all the mustangs were now secured and the chance of any of them escaping was very slim. Tom and Marty had also brought enchiladas and rice from the base camp, plus homemade guacamole with chips and a six-pack of beer in a cooler. Marty, an older man with a bushy white mustache, had been busy laying the food out on a folding table beside the fire while Grace related the accounts of the day—minus what had happened in the truck, of course.

"Once we take these strays back and assess their condition," Tom said when they'd all filled a plate, "we can move the herd to an adoption ranch in Amarillo. Shouldn't take more than four or five days in all, then we can head for home." Tom swiveled a look at his sister. "After this trip, Gracie, that must sound pretty good to you."

Grace glanced up at her brother. She knew him well enough—the tilt of his head, the tone of his voice, the subtle narrowing of his eyes—to read between the lines of his casual comment. Tom wasn't dumb, and he wasn't blind. He knew her just as well as she knew him, and he obviously sensed something was going on between her and Rand.

He wanted a reaction, she knew, but he wasn't going to get one. She was a big girl, after all. The last thing she needed was her brother sticking his nose where it didn't belong. Whatever had happened between her and Rand was her business.

"A long, hot shower would be lovely," she said with a smile, and bit into a chip loaded with spicy guacamole. "I just might feel human again."

"How 'bout you, Rand?" Tom turned his attention to Rand. "You coming to the base camp with us?"

Grace felt her heart jump, then sink when Rand shook his head. Of course he wouldn't come along. He was going on to Wolf River. Which was exactly what he needed to do, she knew. She'd been a fool to hope for even a second that he wouldn't be on his way as soon as possible. And she was selfish to wish for anything different.

Well, so she *was* selfish, dammit. She attacked another chip. So she did want another few days with him. Another few hours, even. Everything between them had happened so quickly, and it wasn't enough. She wanted more.

Much more.

He didn't look at her, and she was glad. After the day they'd had, and as tired and strung out as she felt, she might have started with the tears again. That was all she needed to complete her humiliation. To start crying like a baby not just in front of Rand, but her brother and Marty, as well.

"Grace?"

"What?" She jerked her gaze up at the sound of Tom's voice. She'd been so lost in thought, she hadn't been following the conversation.

"The fund-raiser? You know, the one Mom and Dad are giving for the foundation?"

"What about it?"

He lifted a brow. One of those, so-there-*is*-something-going-on brow lifts. Terrific, she thought with a silent groan, and knew that the ride back to Abilene with her brother was going to be a long one.

"Mom thought you'd want to know that Bradshaw declined the invitation."

"I was hoping that the third time would be a charm," Grace said with a sigh.

She'd known that the man wouldn't come. Bradshaw was one of the wealthiest ranchers in Dallas, and the most mysterious. Rumors ran rampant about the man, from the story that he was disfigured and never went out in public, to the more romantic, though melancholy, version that he'd never left his house after his wife had died years earlier. His age was between twenty-five and seventy-two, based on who was telling the most current version of the man's life. Grace had invited Bradshaw to the last two fund-raisers, but he'd always declined, then sent an eye-popping donation the next day. But if she could get him to actually come to the event in person, she knew that the attendance would double, as would the donations.

She shook her head and shrugged. "I'll try him again next time."

"Dylan Bradshaw?" Rand asked casually. "From the Rocking B?"

Everyone went still and looked at Rand. Even Marty, who'd seen and done most things, Grace knew, looked surprised.

"You know Dylan Bradshaw?" Grace asked.

Rand took a bite of rice. "I know him."

"You mean you've met him," Tom said.

"It's pretty hard to know someone if you haven't met them," Rand pointed out, then added, "We worked together a while back."

Not, *I* worked for *him*, Grace noted. But *we* worked together. She wondered what "a while back" meant, but it would be rude and pushy to start grilling Rand with questions about his past and how he knew Dylan Bradshaw.

"Yeah, well, maybe you could give him a call and get him to change his mind," Tom said with a grin, clearly joking.

"Maybe."

Tom's grin faded. Even Marty had stopped chewing. Grace knew that her brother didn't really believe that Rand could just pick up a phone and get the man to go to the fund-raiser. Still, there was a mixture of awe and disbelief in both Tom's and Marty's eyes that she found extremely humorous.

But whether Rand could or couldn't get Dylan Bradshaw to attend the fund-raiser didn't matter to her. At the moment she wasn't concerned with or interested in any man other than Rand.

If Tom and Marty hadn't driven up when they had this afternoon, he would have made love to her again. It would have been their last time, she thought, knowing that there was no way they could be together now that her brother and Marty had joined them. Her body still tingled from earlier, and she could still feel the texture of his rough hands as they'd slid over her skin and the hard press of his mouth on hers. She was thankful they'd at least had those few hours alone.

She watched him talk with Tom and Marty, saw his expression change from serious, as they discussed the upcoming auction, to smiling, when Marty piped up and told a joke about a cowpoke and an amorous heifer.

All of this should have been perfect, the sun setting in ribbons of reds and golds, the soft nickering from the horses, the ripple of the nearby creek. Talking and laughing around a crackling fire. It *would* be perfect, except for the tiny little detail that the man she loved would be gone from her life by morning.

Damn you, Rand.

Needing to keep busy, Grace offered to clean up after they finished eating. While Rand and Tom settled the horses down for the night, Marty prepared the trailer to haul the mustangs out the next morning.

The frogs were out in full chorus when Grace went down to the creek with a metal bucket. The air had cooled, and a light breeze carried the scent of damp earth and mesquite. She bent to fill her bucket with water when a huge bullfrog jumped in front of her and croaked.

Grace frowned at the frog. "If you think I'm going to kiss you, just forget it, buster. I'm a little sour on fairy tales and happy endings at the moment."

She scooped up water, then stood. When she turned, she bumped into Rand. He reached out a hand to steady her when she stumbled.

"Talking to frogs now?" he asked her with a smile.

She felt her cheeks warm and hoped he hadn't heard what she'd said. But even if he had, she decided, what difference did it make? He already knew how she felt, and like the saying went, once the horse was gone, it didn't do much good to lock the barn door.

"I thought you were with the horses."

"I was. I'm here now."

She rolled her eyes. "I can see that."

There was a long, awkward moment between them. It was obvious that he wanted to say something but didn't quite know how.

With a sigh Grace ran a hand through her hair. "Just say it, Rand. Whatever it is, just say it."

"I'm leaving."

Her chest tightened, as did her grip on the bucket handle. It was one thing to know he was leaving, and another to hear him actually say it. "You mean now?"

"If I get out of here before dark, I can make Wolf River by two or three in the morning."

"Okay." Only it wasn't. It wasn't okay at all.

"Tom and Marty can handle the mustangs without me," he said evenly.

"I'll put some coffee on," she said, surprised that her voice sounded so steady. "You're going to need a thermos if you're driving half the night."

She started past him, but he put his hand on her arm. "Grace—"

She shook her head. "Don't say it, Rand. I'll be all right."

His hand tightened on her arm, and for a moment she thought that he might pull her to him and kiss her. But the sound of her brother's voice had him stepping away.

They walked back to the camp together, and while he loaded his horses she made strong coffee, hoping the extra caffeine would help him stay alert on the long drive across the Texas flatlands at night.

Tom and Marty shook his hand when he was all packed up and ready to go. When he turned to her, she offered her hand to him, as well, though she desperately wanted to throw herself in his arms and give him a kiss goodbye that he'd never forget. Their eyes met for a second, then he let go of her hand and turned away.

She watched numbly as he got in his truck, then started the engine and slowly drove away, his tires crunching over the rocks and debris.

And then he stopped.

He jerked open the door of his truck and walked back toward her. His dark gaze was on her every step of the way.

Her heart pounding, she watched as he marched up to her and stopped.

"Come with me."

That was all he said. *Come with me.*

She knew he just meant to Wolf River. For now that would have to be enough.

She nodded.

Grace saw the relief in Rand's eyes before he turned again and walked back to his truck to wait for her.

"Grace." Tom frowned. "What the hell is going on?"

"I'll be home in a couple of days," she said, releasing the breath she'd been holding. "I'll explain everything then."

Grace kissed her brother and said goodbye to Marty, then grabbed her bag and walked to Rand's truck. She got in and put her seat belt on, then stared straight ahead.

Neither one of them spoke.

In twenty minutes they were back on the highway and headed for Wolf River.

Nine

Rand woke early to the feel of cool, cotton sheets and warm, bare skin. Grace lay beside him in the hotel bed, her long, lovely back turned to him. He rose on one elbow and let his gaze travel slowly over her, the rise of her hip under the sheet, the sexy curve of her shoulder, her delicate, swan-like neck. All those glorious auburn curls fanning across the pillow she currently had her face half-buried in.

He picked one of those curls up and rubbed it between his fingers. Her hair was soft and had a silky quality to it. Without thinking, he brushed the curl against his lips, then frowned at the silly sentiment of it.

Damn, but he was getting soft. Since when did he think about swans and silk?

Must have been about the same time he'd completely lost his sanity and asked Grace to come to Wolf River with him.

He still wasn't certain how it had happened. One minute he'd been driving away, the next thing he knew he was saying, "Come with me."

If he'd have given it time, thought it through, he never would have brought her with him. She had her own life to go back to, her own world. A world he didn't belong in any more than she belonged in his. He had told himself that what had happened between them on the mountain and in the canyon would stay there, that he could leave all that, and her, behind him when it was time to go.

He'd been wrong.

Some strange, unexplainable force had brought them together. He simply accepted that without question, took each day as it came. He had feelings for Grace, as unfamiliar as they were confusing, but he had no delusions about tomorrow or the day after that. He might have lived his life on the edge, but when women were involved, he'd always been careful. And he'd always been honest. No pretense of marriage or babies or happily ever after.

He'd be careful now, too, he told himself. So maybe Grace had gotten to him. Maybe he was a little soft on her. So what? It didn't mean a damn thing. He'd wanted her to come to Wolf River with him. Wanted her to be with him for a little while longer.

He watched her stretch, then roll to her back. The

sheet slipped down, hovered precariously at the peak of her breasts.

Blood shot straight from his brain downward as he stared at her. His pulse pounded in his head.

He couldn't get enough of her. Couldn't stop himself from wanting her. When the time came, he would stop, he told himself. He would leave.

But the time was definitely not now.

She stretched again, and the sheet slipped lower. The pounding in his head increased, as did the ache in his loins. Her skin was pale and smooth, her rosy-tipped breasts full and firm.

He closed his eyes on a silent oath, swore that he'd let her sleep. Lord knew she needed it.

They'd rolled into town sometime around two in the morning and checked into a large, classy-looking hotel called the Four Winds that also had the facilities to care for his horses. Rand himself would have settled for The Silver Saddle Inn they'd passed on the outside of town, but Grace deserved something better than a hard mattress and lumpy pillow in a run-down motel. Grace deserved fluffy down pillows, smooth, satin sheets and room service.

And so many other things that he couldn't give her, too, he thought.

Her eyes fluttered open, and she turned her emerald-green gaze on him. Something shifted in his chest, swelled, then settled back down again.

Smiling, she pulled the sheet up and rolled to her side to face him. "Good morning."

"Mornin'." He grinned at her, tugged the sheet back down again. "I was enjoying the view."

Her cheeks turned pink, and she rolled to her stomach. "Show's over, mister."

"Hardly." He skimmed his hand down the curve of her back, taking the sheet with him as he exposed bare skin. When his hand cupped her bottom and squeezed, he watched her eyes darken with desire.

"You're insatiable," she murmured breathlessly.

"Complaining?" His hand slid lower, over the backs of her thighs. "Just tell me to stop, and I will."

She closed her eyes and stretched as if she were a cat. "I'll get back to you on that."

Chuckling, he explored the soft curves of her long legs and firm, round bottom. She moaned when he skimmed his fingertips along the sensitive skin of her inner thighs, sucked in a breath when he slipped one finger inside the moist heat of her body.

His own breathing was labored, his heart racing, but Rand forced himself to take it slow. They'd made love last night after they'd tumbled, exhausted, into the bed. But from the first time they'd made love by the fire that night, every time for them had been hurried, the need urgent and desperate. He wanted this time to be different.

Slow, he thought. He wanted this time to be slow.

He bent and pressed his lips to her shoulder, nibbled, then used his teeth to pleasure. He felt her shiver and squirm underneath him, but when she started to roll over, he slid his leg over the lower half of her body and held her pressed to the mattress. He kissed her neck, tasting, savoring every inch of smooth, soft skin, used his teeth on every sensitive spot, until she was writhing underneath him.

"Shh," he whispered as he gently bit the lobe of her ear, then slid his tongue inside.

Grace fisted the pillow under her face and buried the sound of her moan in the soft down. What Rand was doing to her was the most erotic, exquisite thing she'd ever experienced. His mouth and lips on her shoulders and neck were driving her mad. And his teeth—she gasped as he nipped lower, scraping and tenderly biting her shoulder blades. He lingered in one especially sensitive area and gave that spot his complete attention.

He was clearly taking his time.

"Rand, please," she begged him.

He straddled her, pressed her deeper into the soft mattress as he slid one hand all the way up her back until his hand fisted in her hair. Her entire body throbbed with raw, sharp need. He moved his free hand over her back and shoulders, and the feel of his rough palm and fingertips on her nerve-wakened skin had her struggling for breath. She couldn't move with him on top of her, yet that didn't frighten her, it only excited her all the more. She belonged to him, she thought. Completely.

With his hand still intertwined in her hair, he bent and kissed her neck again, then slid his free hand under her body to cup her breast. He found her nipple and rubbed the hardened tip between his thumb and forefinger. Intense pleasure shot from that spot to the already aching place between her legs.

She felt the hard length of him pressed against her bottom and thought she might go crazy with wanting him inside her. She moved against him, pleaded, but he barely seemed to notice her anxiety.

She swore at him, but still he took his time.

And then his hand slipped lower, from her breast, down her stomach, then slid lower, to the vee of her legs. When he slid his finger over the aching, throbbing nub of her womanhood, she cried out and arched her body upward. He stroked her, fueled the already out-of-control fire in her body, until she was sobbing his name.

He said something, though her mind couldn't comprehend what it was, then suddenly she was on her back and he was inside her. She reared up and met him, brought him deeply inside her, wrapped her arms and legs tightly around him.

When the climax exploded in her, he muffled the sound of her cry with his mouth, then groaned deeply as he shattered, too.

Unable to think, to speak, or even move, Grace fell back and took him with her.

It was a long time before they moved. A fine sheen of sweat covered both their bodies, and the only sound in the room was the wild beating of their hearts. Rand knew he should move, that he was much too heavy for her, but when he tried to roll away, her arms and legs tightened on him and held him still.

To ease his weight on her, he rose on his elbows, then pressed his temple to hers and kissed the tip of her nose.

"You were…" she said, still breathless. "That was…"

"Pretty damn amazing, Grace," he finished for her.

"Yeah." She smiled, then started to laugh.

It took him a moment to realize what he'd said, then he started to chuckle. She *was* amazing, he thought. He'd never laughed like this in bed with a woman before. This was a whole new experience for him. *Grace* was a new experience for him, as were the feelings he had for her. He'd thought that nothing could surprise him anymore, that he'd seen it all and done most of it, too.

And then Grace came waltzing into his life and turned everything upside down.

He wasn't sure he liked it, but there was nothing to be done about it now. Fool that he was, he couldn't let her go just yet.

But he would, he knew. He'd have to.

She ran her hands over his shoulders, then slid her palms to his chest. The expression on her face turned serious as she lifted her gaze to his.

"When are you going to call the lawyer?" she asked.

He'd known they were going to have to get around to facing that. He'd intentionally kept the lawyer, and the reason they'd come to Wolf River, out of his mind since they'd driven into town. He'd wanted to concentrate on Grace, instead. Wanted to remember the way her cheeks flushed after they'd made love, the soft, dreamy haze in her eyes, the breathy tone of her voice. He wanted to remember everything about her, knew that he'd carry even the smallest detail with him for the rest of his life.

With a sigh he rolled away from her and sat on the edge of the bed. He stared at the phone on the nightstand, felt as if his blood had turned to sludge in his veins. He was afraid if he reached for the receiver that Grace would see his hand shake.

"It's early," he said roughly, and dragged his fingers through his hair.

She rose up on her knees behind him and wrapped her arms around his neck, then pressed a tender kiss to his cheek. "Leave a message, and he'll call you back when he gets into the office."

"After I take a shower."

Her lips moved to his ear and nibbled. "Now."

He frowned, but her hot breath and tongue on his ear made it impossible to be irritated. Or coherent.

He snatched up the phone and punched the hotel operator, then asked her to connect him with Beddingham, Barnes and Stephens Law Offices. He left a brief message on the lawyer's office machine, gave him the phone number at the Four Winds Hotel and the number of the room, then hung up.

His insides coiled, and his heart pounded. But he'd done it. He'd actually made the call.

Grace slid her hands over his shoulders and down his arms, then back up again in a gentle, soothing motion. Slowly he felt his muscles relax and his breathing steady.

"You go ahead and shower." She touched her lips to his shoulder. "I'll order some coffee and breakfast."

He turned suddenly, drew a gasp from her as he stood and swept her up in his arms. His mouth swooped down on hers, and he kissed her hard.

"I've got a better idea," he said, his lips still pressed to hers.

"What is it?" she murmured.

He smiled, then took her into the shower with him and showed her.

"Mr. Sloan, thank you for coming." Henry Barnes welcomed Rand into his office with a warm handshake, extended a hand to Grace. "Miss Sullivan, a pleasure to meet you."

"Mr. Barnes."

"We're informal here in Wolf River," the silver-haired, sixtyish lawyer said, then gestured for both Rand and Grace to sit in the armchairs opposite him. "Just call me Henry."

The smell of leather and freshly polished oak filled the lawyer's office. The carpet was navy blue, the walls oak wainscot, with dozens of certificates of education and awards mixed with various Barnes family photos. Rand noticed a copy of the *Wall Street Journal* on a small corner table, right beside a thick catalog of miniature trains and railroad accessories.

"Rand—may I call you Rand?" Henry asked as he

sat. When Rand nodded, Henry smiled. "You're a difficult man to reach. I was beginning to think I might not hear from you."

From his back pocket Rand pulled out the letter he'd been carrying with him for the past several days and laid it on the lawyer's desk. "Tell me about my sister and brother."

"Of course." The lawyer sat back in his chair. "If I were you, I wouldn't want a bunch of small talk or legal blather, either. So I'll say it as simply and directly as possible. Your brother and sister are alive. Seth, who is now Seth Granger, is living in New Mexico. We haven't heard back from him yet, but we do have an address and it appears to be a reliable one."

Rand had been in El Paso for the past six months. He'd been so close to the border he could have spit and hit New Mexico. He'd driven into Albuquerque at least a dozen times. The thought that he and Seth might have passed on the highway, or even been in a gas station or corner store at the same time, made Rand's pulse jump.

"And Lizzie?" he asked through the thickness in his throat.

"Elizabeth has been more of a problem, I'm afraid."

Rand gripped the arms of his chair, felt a muscle jump in his jaw. He didn't think he could bear it, to come all this way, to get this far, and find out that she didn't want to see him.

"What kind of a problem?" he asked tightly.

"We haven't been able to locate her yet," Henry

said. "We have every confidence that we will, but for the moment, we only know that she's living somewhere on the east coast or, at least, that she was living there."

Rand let out the breath he'd been holding, then narrowed his gaze at the lawyer. "I want to know how this happened and why, after all this time, you're contacting me now."

Expression somber, the lawyer glanced at Grace.

Grace rose. "I'll just wait out—"

Rand took her hand and pulled her back. He wanted her here, with him. As much as it disturbed him, he *needed* her here.

"Whatever you have to say—" Rand kept his gaze on her as he pulled her back onto the chair, then looked back at the lawyer "—Grace can hear, too."

Henry nodded, then let out a long puff of air as he sat forward in his chair. "Twenty-three years ago, in a sudden and violent thunderstorm, your family's car went over the side of a ravine. Your parents were killed instantly, but you, your sister and brother were all still alive."

Rand pressed his lips into a thin line. "Tell me something I don't know, Henry."

"The first person on the scene was the sheriff in Wolf River, a man named Spencer Radick. He called your uncle William, who went to the scene of the accident with his housekeeper, Rosemary Owens."

Rosemary. Rand had forgotten the woman's name until now. She'd told him to call her Rose. He remembered the scent of onions and garlic had clung to her simple brown dress the night she'd taken him to the motel room.

"My uncle sent me with her," Rand said absently. "She took care of me until the other man came and took me to live with the Sloans."

"That other man was Leon Waters," Henry said. "A seedy lawyer from Granite Springs who worked for your uncle. He arranged all the adoptions, but they were illegal, of course. With your uncle's help, Waters also had death certificates forged and paid off all the necessary people to make it appear that the entire family had indeed died. Sheriff Radick was paid for his silence, and he left town two months after the accident, though no one knows where he went. Not long after that, Leon Waters closed up his practice in Granite Springs and disappeared, as well."

The list of people Rand wanted to pay a visit to was quickly growing. And the number-one person on his list was William Blackhawk. "My uncle?"

Henry shook his head. "He died in a small plane crash two years ago."

Anger tore at Rand's insides, a searing, hot rage at the knowledge that he would never be able to face his uncle, to ask him how he could have done what he'd done to his own flesh and blood and still look at himself in the mirror.

Rand narrowed a gaze at the lawyer. "What about the housekeeper? Where can I find her—talk to her?"

Henry shook his head. "She died from lung cancer six months ago."

Grace slipped her hand over his and squeezed. That simple gesture, and the look of concern in her eyes, dispelled the fury and disappointment spilling into his veins.

Rand linked his fingers with hers, then looked back at the lawyer. "If everyone is dead or gone, then how do you know any of this?"

"Rosemary's daughter found a journal detailing everything that happened that night, including names," Henry said. "Rosemary must have kept the journal for her own protection against William. No doubt she feared for her own life."

After what his uncle had done, Rand thought, it was hardly a surprise that the man would be capable of murder if he had felt threatened. Rosemary had been smart to keep a journal as insurance.

Rand was anxious to see that journal. To see the words in black-and-white on the pages, to know every detail of what had happened that night, to his sister and brother.

Still, it felt as if something didn't fit, didn't make sense, and it dawned on him what it was. "But if Rosemary's dead," he asked the lawyer, "then who hired you to find me?"

"Lucas Blackhawk."

"Lucas Blackhawk?"

Henry nodded. "Your cousin."

Rand furrowed his brow. "I have a cousin?"

"Actually, you have two. But for right now, let's talk about Lucas. Your father had two brothers, William and Thomas. Lucas is Thomas's only son. He lives here in Wolf River." Grinning, Henry leaned forward. "Why don't we give him a call and tell him you're here?"

Ten

Lucas Blackhawk's house was a few miles off the main highway, just outside of town. Rand pulled his truck up and parked in front of a pretty, two-story, blue-gray clapboard, with white shutters and trim and an inviting front porch with freshly potted containers of yellow daisies and orange marigolds. Beside the gravel-lined circular drive, there were a pair of child's plastic toy bikes, one pink, one blue. On the corner of the porch, a colorful wind sock of suns, moons and stars danced in the late-afternoon breeze.

Grace looked at the red roses blooming under the porch railing, the neatly manicured green grass and a painted wooden sign stuck into the ground beside the porch steps that said, Welcome. It was like a picture in a magazine advertising the perfect life, a dream home complete with two point three children and the proverbial station wagon.

Her heart swelled just looking at it all. The house, the children's bikes, the homemade welcome sign. She wanted this, too, she realized. All of this, even the flowers and that silly wind sock.

And the kicker was—life's little joke on her—was that she wanted it with a man who'd made it perfectly clear he had no interest in hearth and home or settling down.

She glanced over at him, saw him staring intently at the house, not with yearning but with apprehension. She set her own feelings aside, knew that she'd have plenty of time later to deal with them. Considering everything that was happening in Rand's life, she was being selfish to think about what she wanted.

He hadn't said more than a dozen words for the past hour. Not that being quiet was anything unusual for Rand. But the tension radiating from him had been almost tangible. Grace understood he was still trying to sort through and absorb everything he'd learned about what had happened the night of the accident, how Rand and his sister and brother had been the puppets in his uncle's cruel and sick plan. And now, finding out he had a cousin right here in Wolf River was only more fuel for the fire of turmoil burning inside him.

Though it had been subtle, she'd already felt him pull away from her, not just emotionally, but physically, as well. He hadn't touched her once since they'd left the lawyer's office, and it seemed as if he'd intentionally kept his distance.

Already she felt as if she didn't belong here. That he had too much in his life at the moment, and that she would only complicate matters even more. He'd been impulsive when he'd asked her to come with him, and she'd been impulsive when she'd agreed.

And even knowing all that, it didn't matter. Because if she had to do it all over again, she'd still say yes. She still would have come with him.

She would have gone to Antarctica with him if he'd asked.

She forced a smile on her lips and a light tone to her voice. "Here we are."

He nodded, then got out of the truck and came around to her side. She slid out before he could open her door, and together they walked up the porch steps. From inside the house Grace heard the sound of children screaming in laughter and a woman's voice saying, "I found you!"

Rand hesitated, then knocked on the door.

The door swung open a moment later. A woman, her face flushed and her short crop of pale-blond hair mussed, stood on the other side. Her eyes were smoky blue, large with excitement and pleasure. In her late twenties, Grace guessed.

She was stunning. Absolutely beautiful. And very pregnant, Grace noticed through the loose floral dress the woman wore.

Two point three children, Grace thought with a bittersweet smile. "Lucas!" the woman called over shoulder. "He's here!"

Then she reached for Rand, took his hand in both of hers and pulled him inside the house. Grace followed hesitantly, feeling like an intruder at such a personal, important meeting between Rand and his relatives.

The house was beautiful inside, as well—white walls, shiny hardwood floors, polished oak banister on the stairway. And the intoxicating smell of baking cookies filled the air.

"I'm Julianna." The woman smiled brightly and nodded to her left. Two small children, one boy, one girl, stood perfectly still in the entryway of a dining room. "That's Nicole and Nathan. You can't see them 'cause they're invisible right now."

The children were undoubtedly twins, Grace realized. Probably around three or four, both with dark-brown hair, dressed in jean shorts and white T-shirts. Mischief sparkled in their big, dark eyes.

"Hello, Nicole and Nathan," Rand said, though he intentionally looked at the stairway directly ahead, instead of at the children, and Grace realized that he was actually playing with the children. "It's nice to meet you."

Nathan and Nicole giggled, but when a man dressed in paint-splattered jeans and a navy-blue T-shirt came down the stairs, wiping his hands on a rag, they both ran and jumped on his legs at the bottom step. "Daddy!"

He was a tall man with black hair, both traits obviously dominant in the Blackhawk genes. He was a handsome man—another Blackhawk trait—with deep-brown eyes and a warm smile.

"Just finishing up the trim in the nursery," Lucas said, stuffing the rag into his back pocket. He scooped one child up in each of his arms, kissed both of them, then set them down again. Grinning, Lucas held his hand out to Rand. "Is this the damnedest thing or what?"

"That's putting it mildly."

Grace felt tears burn her eyes when the two men firmly clasped hands. She sensed both Rand's and Lucas's hesitation, their assessment of each other. But she also sensed their excitement, felt it herself as she watched them. Still, they were being cautious with each other, Grace realized, another Blackhawk trait.

"And this is?" Lucas looked at Grace and raised a brow.

"Grace Sullivan." Grace offered her hand to Lucas. "Just a friend."

Lucas and Julianna both shook her hand, then Lucas furrowed his brow. "Grace Sullivan? The same Grace Sullivan with the Edgewater Horse Adoption Agency?"

Surprised that Lucas would know about her and the foundation, Grace hesitated. "Ah, well, yes, I am."

"You sent us an invitation to your fund-raiser next week. I believe my office manager, Shelby Davis, RSVP'd that we'd be there."

Lucas Blackhawk. No wonder the name Blackhawk had sounded so familiar to her. Grace had seen the list of people invited, but she'd been busy trying to track down Rand. Mattie, one of the volunteers with the foundation, had been in charge of organizing the event and handling the guest list.

Even after Rand had told her his birth name was Blackhawk and he'd been born in Wolf River, Grace hadn't connected him with the Blackhawk Ranch. How could she have missed such a blatant link between the two?

But she knew how she'd missed it. Since she'd met Rand, Grace hadn't been thinking clearly. She hadn't been thinking about the foundation or the fund-raiser or anything else besides Rand himself.

Embarrassed and at a complete loss for words, she simply said, "I—I'm so glad you'll be able to attend."

"Why don't you take Rand and Grace into the den, and I'll bring everyone something cold to drink?" Julianna said. With a serious expression on her face, she looked around the room, right past her children, who stood shoulder to shoulder at the foot of the stairs. "If I can find Nicole and Nathan," Julianna said, still searching the room, "I might have some cookies for them in the kitchen."

Grace watched the two children run to their mother, yelling, "Here we are, Mommy. Here we are!" then race off into the kitchen.

There it was again. That little *ping* in her heart. Grace drew in a slow breath to steady herself, then smiled at Rand. "I'm going to see if I can help Julianna in the kitchen. Why don't you and Lucas go on?"

He'd need this time alone with his cousin, Grace understood. From everything the lawyer had told them, Rand and Lucas had a great deal to talk about.

"Take your time," she said, already turning toward the kitchen. "I'm going to see if I can beg a cookie or two from Julianna."

"Beg a few for us, too, will you?" Lucas said as Grace made her way toward the kitchen, then he turned to Rand and grinned. "My wife gains twenty pounds with this baby and puts *me* on a diet. Women."

Rand's thought exactly, as he watched Grace disappear into the kitchen. She'd been acting odd ever since they'd pulled into his cousin's driveway. He'd seen the longing in her eyes as she'd stared at the house, and he hadn't missed the soft, dreamy expression on her face when she'd looked at Lucas and Julianna's twins.

As he followed Lucas into the den, Rand glanced around the house, noticed the toys spilling from a yellow plastic toy box, the wedding photos on the walls, the balls of blue and pink yarn beside the half-knit baby blanket on the leather sofa.

Rand knew it all looked picture-perfect. The house, the kids. Roots. But what did he know about roots? Everything had been ripped out from under him when he was nine years old. Hell, everything he owned would fit in a suitcase, and even his suitcase had wheels.

He couldn't offer any of this to Grace. And she deserved it, all of it.

"I found this in a box of my mother's old photos." Lucas handed Rand a picture shot from an old Polaroid camera. "I thought you might like it."

The picture had faded with age; the edges had turned amber and brown. But clearly the smiling faces of Jonathan and Norah Blackhawk stared back at Rand.

His whole family was in the picture. Rand guessed he was probably around five or six, Seth maybe three or four, and Lizzie, wrapped in a blanket, looked like a newborn. They were all sitting on a hospital bed.

Rand felt as if a metal band were closing around his chest, squeezing every last drop of air from his lungs. He couldn't look at it now, not with Lucas watching him. Rand slipped the picture into the back pocket of his jeans, had to swallow the lump in his throat before he could speak. "Thanks."

"I'm sorry we didn't know each other when we were kids," Lucas said. "Maybe if we had, things would have been different somehow."

There were so many questions racing through Rand's mind at the moment. Why hadn't they known each other? What had happened to Lucas's parents? What did he know about Seth and Lizzie? He didn't know which one to ask first, so he chose the one that he'd been wondering about since he'd left the lawyer's office.

"Why are you doing this?" Rand asked. "Why, after all these years, would you go to all this trouble to bring me and my sister and brother together?"

"Why wouldn't I?" Lucas asked. "You're family. You and your sister and brother."

"You don't even know us," Rand pointed out.

"We're blood, Rand," Lucas said evenly. "I lost my parents when I was young, too. My mom when I was eleven, then my dad not long after that. He died in prison."

"Prison?"

"You would have only been around seven or eight at the time. Both of our families were busy with problems of their own during those years, not to mention our dear uncle William doing his best to cause upheaval wherever he could. He made sure the family stayed divided." Lucas sighed. "William was the only person who could have helped clear my father of the false charges against him. He never returned even one of my father's phone calls. He let my father die in that prison and me be shipped off to foster homes."

"Why?" Rand asked. "Why would a man tear his own family apart like that?"

"His brothers married off the reservation," Lucas said. "He hated them and all their children for that. And then, of course, there was the money."

Rand shook his head. "My parents had no money. We barely got by on a fifty-acre horse ranch."

Lucas turned his head at the sound of the women's laughter from the kitchen, then put a hand on Rand's shoulder and gestured toward the sliding French doors that led to the outside.

"Why don't I show you around my place while we talk?" Lucas said evenly. "This might take a while."

* * *

"You're staying for dinner." Julianna slid a roast into the oven, then set the timer. "I won't take no for an answer."

"I really don't think—"

"I insist." Julianna placed both of her hands on her lower back and stretched. "After being in this house day after day with two three-year-olds, I seriously need an adult to talk to. Just slap my hand if I start to cut your meat for you."

Grace glanced at the two children, who were sitting at their own pint-size table and chairs in a corner of the kitchen, eating chocolate chip cookies and drinking milk. "They're adorable."

"Put cookies in front of them and they're angels." Julianna brought a plate of still-warm cookies to the table and set them down, then slowly eased into a chair across from Grace. "Put carrots in front of them and they turn into little devils so fast your head will spin."

"They're so sweet." Grace accepted a cookie that Julianna offered. "I can't imagine them giving you any trouble."

Julianna gave a bark of laughter. "You should have been here last night. They wanted to see what was inside the vacuum cleaner bag."

Grace's eyes widened.

"And while I was cleaning that up," Julianna went on, "Nicole decided to shampoo Nathan's hair in the middle of my bedroom. Half the bottle was oozing down his face and back, the other half was on the rug. She was on her way for a cup of water when I walked in."

Grace knew nothing about babies or small children. She'd never thought about what kind of mischief they got into, or the destruction they could cause.

But she wanted to know. She wanted to know it all, experience it all. She wanted a dozen of them—well, maybe just three or four, she reconsidered, as the image of vacuum cleaner bags and shampoo popped into her mind.

"At least she used the no-tears," Julianna said with a sigh. "Poor Nathan was screaming he didn't want his hair washed when Lucas tossed them both in the shower. Oh!" Julianna looked down as she smoothed a hand over her stomach. "Soccer time."

Grace followed the rumbling movement across Julianna's stomach. While she had certainly seen a lot of mares ready to foal, Grace had never been quite this close to a woman who was quite this pregnant. Fascinated, she couldn't help but stare. "Does that hurt?"

"Not usually." Julianna winced at the continuing ripple of movement, then frowned at one direct shot to her ribs. "But he's definitely got my attention today."

"You're having a boy?"

"That's what the ultrasound shows." Julianna glanced down at her stomach. "Want to feel?"

Desperately, Grace thought. Not just Julianna's stomach, but she wanted to know for herself, wanted to experience that life growing inside her, a baby with the man she loved.

With Rand.

She might as well wish for the moon.

One prominent bulge on the side of Julianna's stomach moved and popped out directly in the middle. Grace hesitantly held her hand toward that bulge. "You...you really don't mind?"

"Of course not." Julianna took Grace's fingers and laid them directly on top of an undistinguishable baby body part.

When that body part moved under Grace's hand, she felt her breath catch. "He moved!" Grace laughed. "Oh, my heavens, I really felt it!"

Julianna smiled. "I take it you haven't been pregnant."

"No." Though it seemed rude, Grace couldn't bring herself to take her hand away. "I—I'm not married."

"That's not exactly a criterion today," Julianna said, then moved Grace's hand to another bulge. "So what's with you and Rand, then?"

"We, well, we're—" Grace avoided Julianna's eyes. "There's nothing between us."

"Grace, we just met, and you can tell me to butt out of your business anytime. But, honey, I saw the way he looked at you, and the way you looked right back. That's not nothing."

It was strange, Grace thought, how a person could meet someone for the first time yet feel as if they'd been friends for a very long time. That was exactly how she felt about Julianna.

With a sigh Grace reached for a cookie and sat back. "It's complicated."

Julianna laughed. "What relationship between any

man and woman isn't? Lord, someday I'll tell you about Lucas and me, but you better hold on to your eyeballs.''

Grace took a tiny bite of cookie and shook her head. "It's different with Rand and me. You and Lucas obviously love each other very much.''

Julianna absently stroked her stomach, a dreamy, soft expression on her face. "When I don't want to strangle the man for being so pigheaded, I love him so much it hurts.''

"So pigheaded runs in the Blackhawk genes, too, huh?'' Grace said with a smile.

"Lordy, yes. Prepare yourself. The Blackhawk men give new dimension to the word.''

It was too late to prepare herself, Grace thought as she stared at her cookie. Rand was already in her head and in her heart. She'd asked him once how he'd managed after he'd lost his family. He'd told her that life went on. She wasn't sure how it did after you lost someone you love, but she did know she had to believe that was true. Otherwise, she'd end up begging him to at least give them a chance together, to try to love her.

As much as she wanted to do just that, she knew she couldn't. For these past few days she believed that he had truly needed her. She'd been with him as he'd faced the shock of learning his sister and brother were alive, then finding out what had really happened that night, and now, meeting his cousin.

But he didn't need her anymore. He had Lucas and Julianna to help him put the pieces together. And soon he'd have Seth and Lizzie. He'd have his family.

She might have been Rand's lover, but she wasn't his love. He'd made it clear he wasn't looking to settle down. And as she looked at Julianna and Lucas and at their children, Grace knew she couldn't settle for less than that.

It was time for her to go, she realized. Time for her to walk out of Rand's life as abruptly as she'd walked in. In the long run, it would be easier this way for both of them. He might be upset for a little while that she would leave without saying goodbye, but he would probably be relieved, as well. Goodbyes were always awkward. This way there'd be no pretenses that they would stay in touch, no dramatic exits.

And the truth be told, she knew she wasn't brave enough to do it any other way. If she said goodbye to him, to his face, she'd end up in a puddle of tears at his feet. That would only embarrass them both.

Grace forced her attention back to Julianna, but quickly changed the subject back to the twins and the Blackhawk Ranch.

Two cookies and six games of hide-and-seek later, Rand and Lucas still hadn't come back from outside, and Grace knew it was now or never. She swore she felt a migraine coming on and begged off dinner, then asked if Lucas would mind taking Rand back to the hotel later on that evening.

Grace returned Julianna's hug goodbye, then drove back to the hotel in Rand's truck. She packed her bags, left a cheerful note, then on legs that felt like rubber bands, she walked out of the hotel and Rand Blackhawk's life.

Eleven

The town of Wolf River looked different than Rand remembered from his childhood. A glass and brick official U.S. Post Office was now on the corner of Gibson and Main instead of in the back corner of the Rexall drugstore. A multiplex theater showing all the current movies was on Third Street where Drexler's Ice Cream used to be. A popular drive-through hamburger stand with the golden arches was now located directly across from another popular hamburger stand who made eating messy their motto.

Since when did Wolf River need *two* hamburger drive-throughs? Rand thought as he drove down Main Street. He felt a sense of relief when he spotted Papa Pete's Diner on the corner of Main and Sixth. Pappa Pete's made the best food in Wolf River, and on special occasions Rand's family had gone there to eat. On his eighth birthday, Rand remembered, he ordered a hamburger, French fries and a chocolate shake with whipped cream and a bright red cherry on top.

That was the best birthday he'd ever had, he thought with a smile.

There were a few other stores that looked familiar, too. Joe's Barbershop, Peterson's Hay and Feed, King's Hardware. All places Rand's dad had taken him when he was a kid. Places that Rand had forgotten about until now.

He stopped at a red light—something else the town hadn't had twenty-three years ago—and watched as an elderly woman crossed the street and waved at him. Like most small towns, people did that sort of thing. Waved at strangers, held doors for each other, smiled and actually looked you in the eye.

All these years he'd stayed away from Wolf River intentionally. He hadn't wanted to remember the town, the places he'd gone with his family or the people who lived here. Remembering those things couldn't bring his family back to him. Why would he come back?

In all these years he'd never called one place home. Never stayed in one place long enough to "let grass grow under his feet," as the saying went. The minute he started to feel settled somewhere was when he knew it was time to pack up his truck again and hit the road. There was always another ranch, always another horse to train.

Rand turned off Main Street and headed south out of town. The sky was deep blue, the day hot, but he kept his window down and let the wind blow through the cab of his truck as he took in the scenery. There were farmhouses and ranches that he remembered, though he couldn't recall the owners' names. But the names didn't matter. What mattered was that he needed something to hold on to, something with substance to keep him steady when it felt as if his world had been turned upside down.

And now, on top of everything else, Grace was gone, too.

She'd been his touchstone for these past few days. He hadn't realized how much he'd relied on her until she had left. He didn't know he *could* rely on anyone.

His first reaction when he'd come back to the hotel last night and found her gone was astonishment. Had he or someone else said something to her to make her leave without saying goodbye? Had something happened in Dallas and she'd had to get home right away? But her note had been cheery and simple. "I'm sorry I had to leave so quickly, but I really do need to get home and I hate goodbyes."

He'd stood there, staring at the words she'd written, and then the anger had come. He'd sworn, kicked his suitcase and the bed, then he'd slammed around his room and sworn some more. Enough time had passed that she might be home by now, he'd thought, and stomped to the phone to call her, to ask her what the hell she thought she was doing leaving like that.

He slammed the phone back down. He didn't even know her home phone number. He had an office phone number for the foundation, but that was it.

How could that be, he'd asked himself as he'd dragged both hands through his hair. How could they have shared what they had, and he didn't even know her damn telephone number?

He still swore, but there'd been no heat in his words when he'd sunk down on the edge of the bed. He didn't blame her for leaving. She'd given herself completely to him, but he'd given her nothing in return, offered her nothing. Why the hell wouldn't she leave?

He'd gone down to the hotel bar after that. The room was too quiet. Too empty. He thought he needed the company of Jack Daniel's, but two hours and half a bottle later, he knew he'd been wrong.

What he needed was something else entirely.

Rand slammed on the brakes. He'd been so lost in thought he'd nearly missed the turnoff he'd been looking for.

Cold Springs Road.

Hands tight on the wheel, he made a sharp right off the main highway. Oak trees and coyote bush lined the two-lane road. There were no houses out here, the creek bed flooded during storms and the land was too rocky, too unstable to build.

He realized he was driving too fast and he slowed down, forced himself to relax and pay attention to the landscape. It had been so many years, he wasn't certain he would remember.

Soon as the road widens around this turn…

His mother's voice came to him. The sound of thunder and rain on the roof of his parents' car pounded in Rand's head.

We'll be fine...don't be afraid...

There it was. Maybe twenty yards ahead of him. The turn where the road widened.

The turn his father never made that night.

Heart racing, Rand eased his truck off the road and cut the engine. His palms were sweating when he stepped out of his cab and looked down into the ravine.

This is where they'd gone over, he knew. This is where his life had changed twenty-three years ago.

Rand closed his eyes, saw everything again as it had happened that night, the flash of lightning, the car swerving off the road, that horrible sound of silence.

Breathing hard, he opened his eyes and looked around. Overhead, the hot August sun burned through his denim shirt and jeans, and a lazy hawk circled overhead. Puffy white clouds floated on the horizon.

And silence. Absolute, complete silence.

Only, this time the silence didn't frighten him. This silence relaxed and comforted.

Rand turned sideways and dug his boots into the side of the ravine. He slid down standing up; rocks and gravel tumbled ahead of him. A cloud of dust rose from the loosened dirt. At the bottom of the ravine, he looked around again, waited for his heart to slow, then pulled the photograph Lucas had given him from his back pocket.

His family. His only tangible link to the past, he realized. The impact of that knowledge and the importance of what he held in his hand overwhelmed him.

He remembered the day it was taken. Waiting for hours in a small room with his dad and Seth, watching TV and playing games, complaining because he was bored and why couldn't the baby just hurry up and be born?

And then, after she was finally born, they all got to see her, though just long enough for that picture to be taken by one of the nurses. He remembered everything now. The antiseptic smell of the hospital, the squeak of the nurse's shoes on the linoleum, the touch of his mother's lips on his cheek and her words, *Isn't she beautiful, Rand? Do you think you can help me take care of her?*

He'd promised he would. Always and forever, he'd told his mother.

He'd let his mother down. He'd let Lizzie down.

His hand tightened on the photo.

Mary and Matt and Sam had been an important part of his life. Rand was thankful that he'd had them, that he still had them. They were family to him just as much as if they'd shared the same blood.

But his first family needed him now, he knew. And he needed them. Rand had a second chance, a chance to make things right. This time he wouldn't let them down.

They had an address for Seth but not Lizzie. Yesterday the lawyer had asked Rand if he wanted to hire a private investigator to find Lizzie. Rand hadn't given Henry an answer. Lizzie had only been two at the time. What if his sister was happy where she was, with who she was? Would it only complicate her life to suddenly have two brothers she probably didn't remember show up at her doorstep?

But Rand knew that the decision had already been made, that there'd never really been a decision. Lizzie would be contacted by the P.I. who would tell her everything that had happened. Rand wouldn't force himself into her life, or Seth's, either. They'd both be given a choice if they wanted to meet. After that... well, they'd just have to take it one step at a time.

The silence in the ravine surrounded him. In the midst of the stillness, a soft breeze rose, whispered to him. *You'll be fine...don't be afraid...*

Rand listened to the breeze, felt it float over him like a velvet hand. He smiled, then slipped the photo back into his pocket and hurried up the ravine.

What he needed to do now had nothing to do with Seth and Lizzie. What he needed to do now was for himself.

Wearing a black velvet slip dress with V-neckline, spaghetti straps and a slit halfway up her leg, Grace stood outside the open French doors on her parents' brick patio and sipped her glass of champagne. Inside the house, the fund-raising party for the foundation was already in full swing.

By Texas standards, it was a pleasant evening, and Grace had stepped outside for a moment to take a few deep breaths of the warm night air and prepare herself for a very busy night ahead of her.

Normally she thrived on these affairs, knowing that

the money raised would help care for and find homes for so many horses. But nothing seemed normal to her since she'd come back to Dallas. Everything felt different. *She* felt different.

With a sigh Grace glanced across the patio and stared at the wavering pale-blue water in her parents' lit swimming pool.

She felt empty.

"Gracie, darlin', for heaven's sake," Roanna Sullivan said from the open doorway, "if that face of yours hangs any lower, y'all will be kissing your own behind."

It was her mother's favorite reprimand when Grace had been growing up, and, as a child, the silly expression had made her laugh. At the moment, however, Grace did not feel like laughing. However, to please her mother and the 150 guests laughing and talking and eating hors d'oeuvres inside the house, she did plaster a smile on her face.

Roanna—Ronnie to her husband and friends—cocked her head and looked at Grace thoughtfully. "Hmm. Can't decide which I prefer—the tick-fevered bloodhound expression or the I-just-ate-a-sour-apple look."

"You look beautiful tonight, Mom," Grace said, not only to change the conversation, but because it was true. She wore a long, silvery-green off-the-shoulder gown that complemented her short, pale-blond hair, sea-green eyes and slender figure. Even at fifty, the woman still turned heads and made men trip over their tongues and feet.

"Thank you," her mother said. "You look stunning yourself. Now tell me why you haven't smiled once since you got back from your trip."

So much for changing the subject.

Grace sipped from the glass of Dom Pérignon in her hand, though it might as well have been apple juice for all she noticed. "Don't you have to check on the pâté? I heard that you were almost out of it."

Normally a comment like that would have Roanna—a born-and-bred Georgia debutante—dashing away in horror at the mere possibility of such a social faux pas. Tonight she wasn't buying it.

"Gracie." The teasing tone in her mother's voice was gone now. "You've been back five days. When are you going to tell me what happened?"

Five days. God, had it really only been five days? Grace thought. It felt more like five years.

Glancing away from her mother, Grace looked over the sea of shimmering gowns and broad-shouldered tuxedos in her parents' football-field-size living room. From a quartet in one corner of the room, strains of Mozart drifted over the buzz of conversation. Huge bouquets of red and yellow roses and white lilies scented the room and white-gloved servers with silver trays offered mushroom-cheese pastry puffs and salmon mousse toast squares.

A beautiful sight of elegance and wealth and privilege.

And Grace would trade it all in a heartbeat for canned chili over a campfire and one more night on a mountaintop with Rand Blackhawk.

She still felt that leaving the way she did was for the best. It would have been humiliating to burst into tears in the middle of saying goodbye, and would have only made Rand uncomfortable. So she'd made it easier for both of them.

She took another sip of champagne at the thought. Easy. Yeah, right. Leaving had been anything but easy. It had been the hardest thing she'd ever done in her life.

All the way from Wolf River back to Dallas, in the back seat of the car she'd hired through the hotel to drive her home, Grace had alternated between tears and rousing pep talks. *I'm still young,* she'd told herself. *I'll meet someone else. We were too different, I'm better off without him.*

Oh, and her favorite, *It's better to have loved and lost, than never to have loved at all.*

That was a big, fat crock. It *hurt* like hell, dammit.

And, fool that she was, she'd held on to the tiniest sliver of hope. Prayed that he might miss her even a little, that he might call, even to just say hello.

But he hadn't, and she knew she did have to move on. She hoped that everything went well for him, that he would reunite with his family and be happy. Because she loved him, she wanted him to be happy.

Grace felt her mother's gaze still on her, watching her, still waiting for an answer to her question about what had happened. Suddenly thankful that she had her family, her mother and father and brother, she gave her mother a hug.

"Later, Mom," Grace said. "Just you and me, in

the den, pj's and hot cocoa. Then I'll tell you everything."

"Hot cocoa, huh?" Concern narrowed Roanna's eyes as she touched her daughter's cheek. "Must be serious."

Inside the house, it seemed as if the room had quieted. A low hum, like bees in a hive, filled the house. Both Roanna and Grace turned to see what the buzz was about. A handsome dark-haired man at least two inches taller than anyone else in the room, wearing a black Stetson with a black tuxedo, was in the center of all that attention.

"Heavens." Roanna lifted one brow. "Who is *that?*"

Grace stared, dumbstruck. Though she'd never met the man, she knew exactly who it was.

"I'll be damned," Grace said out loud. "He did it. He actually did it."

"Who did what, dear?" her mother asked, her attention still on the man.

"Never mind." Grace turned toward her mother and kissed her cheek. "Go say hello to Mr. Dylan Bradshaw, Mom."

Roanna's eyes widened, then she smiled that devastating smile of hers and squared her shoulders. "Let's see if the man's checkbook is as big as he is, shall we?"

"You go ahead," Grace said. "I'll be there in a minute."

So Rand *had* called the man, Grace thought in wonder, as she watched her mother move through the crowded room in Bradshaw's direction. Even with everything Rand had going on in Wolf River with the lawyer and Lucas and his family, he'd still remembered to make that call. Maybe he'd thought it was the least he could do for her. Sort of a final goodbye gift.

Odd, how a person could feel happy yet so miserable at the same time.

With a sigh she stared at her glass of champagne and knew that as corny as it sounded, it was also true. It *was* better to have loved and lost, than never to have loved at all.

In spite of all the pain and the heartache, she wouldn't have changed one thing that had happened between them. If she didn't have Rand, she would still have the memories. Every touch, every kiss, every laugh they'd shared, she would always remember. Maybe—and it was a big maybe—there would be other men in her life, but no man would ever take his place. No man could come close.

"Miss Grace?"

Startled, she glanced up at Jeffrey's call. Jeffrey, an elderly man with a British accent, had been the Sullivans' family butler since Grace was a little girl. He was more like an uncle than an employee, and Grace adored him.

"You have a package," Jeffrey said in that deep baritone voice of his.

"Would you mind putting it in the study for me?" she asked. "I'll take care of it later."

Jeffrey—the calmest, most composed man on the

face of the earth, hesitated. "I don't believe the study would be an appropriate place to put it, Miss. Nor do I believe you should wait until later."

Grace shook her head. Jeffrey was much too formal, she thought. Not once in all her life had she seen the man let his hair down, so to speak, do the boogie-woogie or shake a tail feather. Life was just too damn short not to enjoy every moment.

Well, dammit, if it killed her, she was going to have a good time tonight. When the music changed later to something fast and fun, she intended to get out there and shake a tail feather of her own.

She might even shock Jeffrey and drag him out there with her.

For the moment, though, she would humor the man. She followed him to the front door, where he surprised her by taking the glass of champagne from her hands, then opened the door for her.

Her surprise turned to shock.

On her parents' front porch, were two foals. And not just *any* foals, but the foals that she and Rand had rescued from Black River Canyon. They bumped nervously into each other, but a lead line and bridle held them in place. Grace stepped outside, followed the ropes attached to those bridles to see who was holding them.

Rand.

Wearing a black tuxedo, of all things, he stood to the side of the front door, leaning casually against the house.

Grace felt her heart leap in her throat.

"Rand," she whispered his name. "What...what are you doing here?"

"Lucas and Julianna couldn't make it," he said. "They sent me in their place."

"Oh." What was she supposed to say? I'm so glad they couldn't come, and would you just please kiss me? "I...I hope everything is all right."

"Everything is great. Julianna had her baby early this morning, two weeks early, but she and the baby are both fine."

"I'm so glad." And she was, Grace thought, her mind reeling. Extremely glad. But with Rand staring at her with those black eyes of his, a smile lifting one corner of his mouth, looking incredibly and ruggedly handsome in the tux he had on, Grace simply couldn't keep a thought straight.

She'd thought she would never see him again, and here he was, standing two feet away from her. She stared at him, held her hands carefully at her sides because she was afraid she was going to leap into his arms and make a complete fool out of herself.

He was here for Lucas and Julianna, Grace reminded herself. Not for her.

She struggled to draw air into her lungs. "What are you doing here with the foals?"

"I adopted them."

"You adopted them?"

He nodded. "And the mares and stallion, too."

"You adopted *all* of them?"

"Yep."

Yep? He'd adopted five horses and all he could say

was "Yep?" The man was enough to make to her crazy. In fact, he already had.

"You said your mother was selling the ranch and all her horses," she said carefully. "Where will you keep them, and who's going to take care of them?"

"Actually—" he pushed away from the wall of the house and moved closer to her "—I was hoping you would."

"Me? You mean the foundation?"

"No. I meant you."

Confused, she looked at the foals. With their big, dark, watery eyes and sweet faces, she tried to think of a way she could keep them, but there wasn't. "Rand, I don't have a permanent place to keep them. That's why they're adopted out, to give them homes."

"What if you did have a place? A permanent place." He moved in front of her and stared down at her. "With me."

"Permanent?" Her pulse skipped, then starting to race. "With you?"

She knew she sounded like a silly parrot, repeating everything he said, but it was the best she could do under the circumstances.

"Yeah. With me." He touched her cheek with his fingertip. "I've got fifty acres in Wolf River. My parents' land. It's not much, but we can buy more later, after we build a new house."

"We?" she barely managed to get the single word out. "You and me, Grace," he said quietly. "A herd of horses, a passel of kids. Maybe even a dog and cat. I always wanted a dog.''

A passel of kids? Terrified that her knees would give out on her, she grabbed hold of his arms and leveled her gaze with his. ''Whatever it is you're getting at, Rand Blackhawk, *will you just say it?*''

He cupped her chin in his hand and looked down at her. ''I'm asking you to marry me, Grace Sullivan.''

Rand watched Grace's eyes widen and felt her jaw go slack in his palm. He'd expected her to be surprised, but hell, no one was more surprised than him.

She blinked, then stepped back from him. ''You're asking me to *marry* you?''

Rand had never done this before, but still, he didn't think that her response was what anyone would call encouraging. He dragged a hand through his hair and frowned. ''Look, I know I won't be the easiest person to live with, but I love you, dammit, so that's gotta mean something.''

''That's how you propose to me?'' she asked, folding her arms. '''I always wanted a dog. I love you, dammit'?''

''Yes.'' That wasn't what he'd intended. Somehow, that's just how it came out. ''So what's your answer?''

''Yes.''

She had him so damn flustered he wasn't certain what she was saying yes to. ''Yes, what?''

''Yes, dammit. I'll marry you.''

''Thank God,'' he said on a rush of breath, then dragged her to him and caught her mouth with his. Laughing, her arms came around his neck, and she kissed him back. He lifted her off the ground, smiled against her lips. "Thank God," he said again, and held her tightly to him. "Thank God."

He deepened the kiss, felt a fierce and powerful emotion grip him. He'd never felt anything like it before, not before Grace, but he knew what it was. Love. He knew that she was his one true love, the woman he wanted to spend the rest of his life with.

"Tell me you love me," he whispered against her mouth.

"I love you," she said, breathless. "I love you, I love you."

She inched away from him and gazed up at him. "What happened in Wolf River, Rand? When I left, I thought I'd never see you again."

On a sigh he touched his forehead to hers. "For the past twenty-three years I've felt guilty. Not only because I hadn't died with my family, but because deep inside of me I was *glad* that I hadn't died. I felt I'd let my family down because I was happy I was still alive. So I didn't believe that I deserved love, and I could never allow myself to love anyone back."

He brushed his lips against hers and smiled. "And then you came into my life, Miss Grace. I'll never forget the way you looked that first day I met you, standing in that hot, dusty barn in your business suit and high heels. I wanted you so bad I hurt."

"That first day?" She frowned at him. "You acted like all you wanted to do was get rid of me."

"I did," he said honestly. "Because I knew you were a threat to me. I knew I was looking at a woman—*the* woman—who had the power to get inside me. The power to make me feel. I'd spent a lifetime not allowing myself to feel, Grace. You scared the hell out of me.''

''You scared me, too,'' she admitted.

''But you didn't back down,'' he said. ''You hung in there, stood up to me, and stuck it out. I'd never met anyone like you before. You absolutely staggered me. You still do.''

There were tears in her eyes as she kissed him, and when she drew back, she smiled at him. ''And you mean it, about the fifty acres and horses and kids and everything? You really want all that?''

''Yeah, I really want all that,'' he said softly. ''But only with you, Grace. Without you, none of it would mean anything to me.'' He grinned at her. ''Not even the five million dollars I just found out I inherited.''

Her eyes widened. ''Five...*million*...dollars?''

''Yep.'' He was still trying to get used to it himself. ''Seems my grandfather had a lot of money he'd made in oil and bonds and put in trust for his children. Since my uncle was the executor, he forged a new will when my grandfather died and took everything.''

''And your parents died without any of what was rightfully theirs,'' Grace said sadly.

''The money didn't matter. My parents died happy, with each other. That was worth more than any amount of money.'' He pressed a quick kiss to her nose. ''But don't get me wrong, darlin'. I intend to enjoy my inheritance. Build a ranch and a house and keep you living in the manner to which you're accustomed."

She frowned at him. "I would have lived in a pup tent if you'd asked me to, buster, though I should tell you I have a healthy trust fund myself, also from my grandparents. We wouldn't have needed to clip coupons to survive."

"Yeah?" He lifted a brow. "I should have married you that first day and saved a lot of time."

"Yes, you should have," she said primly, then the amusement in her eyes turned to concern. "What about Seth and Lizzie?" she asked. "Have you found them?"

"We think we're close to finding Seth, but we've had to hire a private investigator to find Lizzie. They will both be free to do whatever they want with their trust funds, when and if we do actually find them, that is."

"If? You mean you might not find them?"

"We never know what tomorrow brings, Grace." He pulled her into his arms and kissed her again. "But with you by my side, sweetheart, I'm going to look forward to each and every day."

The foals nudged Rand from behind, pushing him closer to Grace. Laughing, he pulled her into his arms and kissed her. "Did I tell you how sexy you look in that dress you're wearing?" he murmured.

"You look pretty damn good yourself in that tux, Blackhawk."

He nuzzled her ear. "So how long before this shindig is over and we can both get naked?"

"Soon," she whispered, then wrapped her arms around his neck and gave him a long, searing kiss that surely must have made smoke come out of his ears.

He whispered what he wanted to do to her later, felt her shudder in response to his words. Later he knew he would make her shudder again and again. And she would do the same for him.

Smiling, he held her close. It had taken him twenty-three years and the love of a special woman, but with absolute certainty, Rand Blackhawk knew that he had finally come home.

*   *   *   *   *

Don't miss IN BLACKHAWK'S BED, the next title in this ongoing series, on sale July 2002